THE BODY IMAGE WORKBOOK FOR TEENS

How Love Yourself, Celebrate your Body, and
Boost Your Self-Esteem to Stress Reduction,
Shyness and Social Anxiety.

By

NAOMI RANDALL

About The Author

Naomi Randall is a teacher, an author and an advocate for women's rights who is originally from Dallas, Texas and who has lived for the past 25 years in a small coastal community in California, with her husband, two children, and one excitable Labrador.

Naomi Randall's interest in fairness and in particular the difficulties that women face in the workplace and with their image compelled her to investigate and research the subject, eventually leading her to write books on the subject that she hopes will help others.

In her free time, Naomi Randall enjoys swimming or surfing in the sea and walking in the hills that are near her home. She loves relaxing with friends, either at the beach or by having a barbecue in her garden, and enjoys drives along the coast when she gets time.

Table Of Contents

INTRODUCTION

Over the years, the media's topic of using girls who are very thin and not fit has not changed, although the complications it creates for teenage girls have been well known.

The media takes a significant part in the picture of the body of a teen. Usually, ads in teen magazines and teen television glamorize items that do not reflect the normal person. In total, today's female models weigh 23 percent less than the average woman.

Per year, the average young person in the United States sees between 13,000 to 30,000 ads on television alone and probably hundreds more a day from magazines, billboards, and the internet.1 The teenager may get the wrong message about body image way too often with all that exposure.

Media targeting young girls appears to emphasize the definition of attractiveness as thinness. It is easy to see that this poses a huge health danger for teenage girls if you try to think that the average height and weight for a model are 5'10 "and 110 pounds, and the height and weight for the average woman are 5'4" and 145 pounds.

Thinness is also glamorized by reality programs, movies, and other popular culture aspects as the ideal of attractiveness. Popular media also depicts only slender people and shows no representation of all forms, shapes, and sizes of the body. Such representations can lead to concerns with the body and, possibly, eating disorders.

Body Image

The teenage phase is a time when it can be extremely harmful to be subjected to these texts. The onset of puberty and the resulting physical changes brought on by this development period will lead to feelings of vulnerability and negative body image.

It is crucial to remember that this is not resistant to boys. Parents need to be mindful that boys will still have difficulties with body image, whether those concerns center on weight, musculature or some other standard of internalized appearance.

It is also important that your child is allowed to watch shows featuring characters who look like them. The way to go is to show that the children look like your teens and their peers with normal body weights. Demonstrate that average is represented as the true average.

Understanding Negative Body Images And Overcoming Them

How many days do you look in the mirror and think, "If I could only lose 10 pounds, I'd be satisfied," then? Unfortunately, the bulk of American women and girls feel unsatisfied with their bodies, and to alter their bodies, many take drastic steps. For example, one study showed that weight was described as the primary factor in deciding how they felt about themselves by 63 percent of female participants-more significant than family, education, or work. Other data shows that 86% of all women want to lose weight and are disappointed with their bodies.

Height, just like weight, is regarded by women and teenage girls as a definitive aspect of their personality. Some girls believe that because they do not fit consistently into "normal" size, there is something wrong about their bodies; others will refuse a pair of jeans merely because they cannot wear a certain size. To assess their self-worth, most girls walk on the scale; if they have lost weight, then it is a positive day, and they will feel 'okay' about themselves temporarily. If the number has only risen too marginally on the meter, then the day is wasted, and they feel useless.

The body image has now been synonymous with one's weight, and thus, if women are not content with their weight, their bodies may not be fulfilled. Sadly, girls and women take things a step further and rationalize that the negative picture of the body is directly equated with self-image. We are now living in a world where young girls think that losing weight and being slim is the only way to boost their self-image and become more secure.

In a culture where their bodies decide who they are, women and young girls now live. Girls are afraid of gaining weight and are constantly reminded by the news of different new food items on the market and the importance of weight loss. Countless television shows often bombard them with plastic surgery, and every year the number of cosmetic procedures is rising in this region. When watching tv, watching a movie, or viewing a magazine, women today face impossible images of beauty every day. Young girls are reported to be exposed to 400 to 600 media photographs every day. Young girls and women inevitably feel uncomfortable about their bodies and physical appearance and frequently find that they must change their bodies to achieve self-esteem. A recent study showed that only 2 % of women worldwide would identify themselves as "beautiful." The vast majority of girls want different facets of their beauty to improve. Self-esteem and body-esteem have been the same in today's culture. Unfortunately, this takes an emotional effect on adolescent people because to exploit their bodies to "fit into" an artificial ideal of appearance, they feel insufficient because they frequently resort to severe habits.

Under this beauty-driven culture, eating disorders have flourished. Young girls and women are swept up in a toxic spiral of resentment of the body. Especially susceptible to this toxic body image pattern are people with eating disorders.

Although a vast number of women are uncomfortable with their bodies, many women and girls face extreme issues with self-confidence that may be part of more complex problems. Shape dysmorphic disorder, eating disorders, and intense depression comprise these extreme body perception disturbances.

Image Dysmorphic Disorder: This is an "imagined ugliness" disorder. A grossly skewed image of what they look like is what people with this disorder see in the mirror. These people will also spend hours analyzing, trying to hide, or obsessing about their supposed weaknesses. To change their bodies, certain persons expend thousands of dollars on cosmetic surgery.

Anorexia Nervosa: An intense apprehension of weight gain characterizes this condition, and some people view their bodies as heavier or "fat" even though they are grossly underweight.

Bulimia Nervosa: People with this disease are also very uncomfortable with their bodies and are highly concerned about body weight and shape.

Depression: People with depression also have a warped image of themselves in certain cases and feel less appealing than they are.

Since unhealthy body image for many women and girls is a widespread issue and may also be a part of many serious disorders, women need to learn to adjust their body image to a healthier and optimistic view of themselves.

Seven Ways Of Overcoming Negative Images Of The Body

1. Fight of "Fatism."

Work on embracing persons of all sizes and types. This will make you love the body you possess. Creating a list of individuals you respect who may not have "full" bodies can be helpful. Can how you feel about the influence of their appearance? It is also important to note that, over the past 50 years, the expectations of culture have changed dramatically. "The ladies who in the 1940s and 1950s were called the" ideal beauties, "such as Marilyn Monroe (size 14) and Mae West, were full-bodied and truly attractive, but by today's standards, they will be called" overweight.

2. Battle the Downfall diet

At any stage of their lives, ninety percent of all women eat, and at some point in time, 50 percent of women feed. A new study showed that to lose weight, 14 percent of five-year-old girls say that they "go on diets." Eighty percent mention being on a diet by the time girls are ten years old. Women are two times more likely than men to die. To the dismay of dieters, after five years, 98% of all dieters recover weight. Studies further demonstrate that 20-25% of dieters are transitioning to a partial or full-blown eating disorder.

Research has found that they feel negative feelings when restrained eaters are subjected to ads linked to food, weight loss, or exercise and are more likely to overeat. If they think that dieting would help them feel better for themselves, women are stupid. Dieting makes you lose your vitality and self-esteem. Mood swings and thoughts of hopelessness are often created by dieting. An intuitive eating strategy can be incredibly effective in overcoming diet loss.

This method emphasizes moderating all food styles and not counting calories or reading labels. Food is "just food" and is not numbered "positive" or "evil." Customers learn to monitor their hunger/fullness and enjoy a balanced food relationship. Speak to a friend or loved one, or get professional support if you feel pressure to lose weight. Many useful books concentrate on feeding intuitively and can be a valuable resource.

3. Genetics Embrace

Remembering so certain parts of the body should not be altered is essential. Genetics play a part in your body, and your chromosomes decide at least 25 percent to 70 percent of your body. Although we cannot alter many parts of your body, you can alter or change your values and perceptions that affect the way you feel about yourself. For you, transformation begins-it is inward, and it begins with self-respect and a good outlook. Focusing on health and not size is critical. It is important not to equate your body with your mates, family members, or photos in the media. All of us are special, and no two bodies are alike. If we "diet into" a new body, we can't be happy or healthy.

4. Know that Emotions are Skin Deep

Discovering the emotions and feelings that underlie your negative image of the body is important. And if you are overweight, the sentence 'I feel fat' is never really about obesity. Any time a woman looks at herself in the mirror and thinks, "Ugh, I'm obese and ugly," she thinks, "There's something wrong with me or with what I see." We turn to our bodies and blame our emotions because we don't know how to cope with our emotions. You betray your body each time you say, "I'm overweight," and you betray and disregard your underlying feelings. Notice that "fat" is never a sensation; it is the avoidance of emotions. Learn to discover your thoughts and thoughts and know that dwelling on your body only distracts you from what "actually" disturbs you.

5. Question Messages Portrayed in the media

By the media, girls and women are given strong messages about their bodies' acceptability or unacceptability. Young girls are taught to equate themselves in the media with women depicted as good, judging how closely they relate to the "ideal" body shape. Sadly, the majority of girls and women (96 percent) do not complement the models and actresses portrayed in the mainstream. The average model is 5'10 "and 110 pounds, while the average girl is 5'4" and 144 pounds. This is the greatest disparity between women and cultural values that has ever existed. This disparity causes many women and girls to believe like their bodies are weak and derogatory. It is necessary to note that only 4 % of women genetically have the "ideal" body portrayed in the media. To achieve this unobtainable portrait, the other 96 percent of women believe they have to go to drastic steps. Many of the photographs presented in the media have been improved and airbrushed by computers. The models' hips and waists were always small, and their breasts were inflated by digital photo editing. Many of the women featured in the media suffer from an eating disorder or have adopted disordered eating patterns to sustain such low body weights. It is necessary to begin to challenge cultural representations and ask why people should feel obligated to "live up" to these artificial expectations of appearance and thinness. In their magazine, one curious side notes: Glamour magazine attempted to use more "normal height" models and discovered that ratings went down. Interestingly, data indicates that women report feeling better towards their bodies after viewing normal photos of women in the media, but this did not increase readership for Glamour magazine.

6. Recognize Body Misperception's impact

Women are more vulnerable than men having more pessimistic thoughts towards their bodies. Females are more physically involved in their body image in general. How you feel about yourself is key to your body image. Research suggests that the product of how positive or negative your body image is 1/4 of your self-esteem. Unfortunately, a higher proportion of their esteem is spent in their bodies by many women with eating disorders. Women with eating disorders can frequently show unequivocal misperception of the body image, of which they misperceive the scale of the whole body portion. They are, therefore, "blind" to their statistics. This illusion is genuine, and it is attributed not to "fat," but to the epidemic of the eating disorder. This misperception must be understood and linked to an eating disorder. Remind yourself that when you feel overweight, you underestimate your form. Before you can trust your new and more reliable self-perceptions, judge your size according to trusted people's views.

7. Your Body Befriend

Combating unrealistic body perceptions is crucial, and in interpersonal relationships, it can lead to depression, shyness, social anxiety, and self-consciousness. Bad body perception can contribute to an eating disorder, as well. It is time for women to avoid negatively criticizing their bodies and respecting their inner self, mind, and spirit. The body of a woman is a marvel of biology; women can menstruate, ovulate, and create life. Start to understand that you should not need to equate yourself in the media with other girls or older women. Start to challenge the media's representations and understand that the meaning of these unrealistic images does not depend on how closely you match them.

Body Wars by *Margo Maine* teaches women to regain control of their bodies and suggests ways to help women enjoy their bodies. Examples of 10 ways you can enjoy your body:

1. It's perfect the way that it is. Your body is fine.

2. It's a powerful weapon. Think about your body. Build an inventory of all the stuff you can do with it.

3. It should give you pride; it shows who you are as a person. Don't think of your size. Walk with your head up.

4. Build a list of individuals who have contributed to your life. How has their appearance helped to achieve their success?

5. Your size shouldn't make decisions for you. Do what you like to do, no matter what.

6. Stop looking in the mirror and stressing over your looks. Replace this time with constructive and enjoyable activities.

7. Let your inner elegance and individuality shine. Show your personality on the outside.

8. Look back to a time in your life when you loved your body and remember those emotions and the confidence you felt. Bring those feelings into your life now.

9. Love your body and work with it as it changes. Don't' fight it.

Oh. 10. Beauty is not skin-deep. It is a representation of yourself as a whole. Love the person inside and enjoy it.

In conclusion, the negative picture of the body is a significant concern and has adverse impacts on women's self-esteem. It can result in anxiety, as well as an eating disorder. Changing the world of ours begins with you—self-love and reverence, beginning with one human at a time, and the end of bigotry. By keeping you away from the inner-self-the spirit, the mind, and the entire true self, the outward pursuit of altering the body will also injure spirituality. Please seek psychological treatment to interrupt the cycle of body hatred if you or someone you care for struggles with a poor body image.

Getting a Professional's Advice

In people with eating disorders, body image is especially difficult to treat. Several principles can aid clinicians with body image disorders with their treatment of women. Evaluating the degree of unhealthy body perception current is useful first. An example of how this can be achieved is by making women draw a front and side profile of their body and then mark various colors the places of affection, want, dislike, and hate. Process each area with the client to demonstrate to her that she thinks that way about each area.

Negative body image disorders have also resulted from past bullying encounters, and young girls and women have advised them to rely on negative remarks from family and peers. I had a 17-year-old client, for instance, who was repeatedly mocked with "chubby cheeks." Her cheeks were sunken because she was anorexic, and she figured her family would eventually tolerate her and avoid bullying her. Before she could consider getting her cheeks, counseling had to work on her childhood bullying.

Another useful step is to assess how much the negative perception of the body affects their daily lives. Some women stop wearing a selection of garments and use clothing to cover their bodies as well. For instance, many customers would wear huge baggy sweatshirts all year long to prevent exposing their stomachs. To shield themselves from a negative body picture, women often postpone practices. For over a decade, many clients have not been to a swimming pool. It can slowly help them accept their bodies by making clients get to confront their worries and "stop avoiding." Encourage consumers to do new stuff to discover their true selves and share it.

Having women exercise proper self-care is also beneficial. This ensures that proper sleep, food, and exercise are important for them. People with eating disorders often feel so negative towards their bodies that they stop caring about themselves, and a negative downward spiral tends to be generated by this self-neglect. Encourage clients to re-engage in behaviors because of their bodies that they have been neglecting.

Help Build A Positive Body Image For Your Daughter

"I have nothing to wear that doesn't make me look disgusting!"
"I'm overweight!" "I'm hideous!"

You can't seem to get through to your daughter, despite all your pep discussions and positive reinforcement. With her presence, she's disappointed and persuaded that someone else is looking at her with judgment. You're sorry that she's so focused on her physical image and, secondly, she doesn't notice her special beauty. How are you helping to build a positive body image for your daughter?

From the inside comes positive self-esteem. As much as we would like to be able to spill it out like a bucket onto our baby, it's not that easy. However, there are ways we can support as parents.

Studies suggest a more favorable body picture for girls who play sports than for girls who don't. To learn to value their bodies and what they can do, girls need to play sports or do another tough physical exercise rather than simply what they look like. It's really important here. How about martial arts, ballet, or dance if your daughter isn't into basketball or tennis? Self-esteem is constructed to learn to bear oneself with confidence and an increasing sense of success as one faces obstacles.

Try an examination of facts. For your daughter, look at modeling magazines and chat about how the images are airbrushed and how a team of professionals makes up the models. The truth is, when she gets up in the morning, no fashion model or actress looks like that! Help her realize that they are not "actual" pictures. You may want to put a cap on the number of those magazines that you encourage your daughter to read. They may negatively affect the self-image of a young woman.

Emphasize effective oversight of wellness. Not every type has the genetics to be a size 2, but with a size 12, you will be safe and feel amazing. Taking good care of our hair and skin causes us to shine from the inside. Instead of comparing themselves to others, girls must learn their comfortable weight and value themselves for who they are. Your daughter will further maximize her natural properties by stressing diet and exercise. Good and satisfied people are still in style.

Support her pick out clothes for her body that are flattering. The girls want to wear what all the others wear. Unfortunately, not all cuts are made for all sizes and types of the body. Find some nice books that teach you how to dress up with your body type at the library. It also makes you look the best by wearing the right colors for the skin tone, hair, and eye color.

When you are focusing on creating your daughter's reputation, warn her brothers and father that they will not tolerate bullying, name-calling, and rude remarks about the appearance of their child. Stop viewing television programs and movies that stress too much body appearance or encourage a negative approach to women and their bodies.

Finally, as a family, institute a workout/balanced food regimen if your teen is overweight. Start going with her for walks or rides, begin a sport together, attend a gym for women only. And before the weight begins to come off, being healthy and regularly exercising improves the mood and promotes more exercise, establishing a positive loop. In our thin, obsessed world, an overweight teen would have a poor self-image. Act as a family together-it will help your teenage daughter build a positive self-image for a long time.

Body Image and Creative Expression

It's not just about "looking healthy" or eating disorders; the body's appearance contributes to our personality and how we think of and embrace ourselves, which explicitly or implicitly influences how we obtain the consciousness and emotional resources that we need to develop.

In entertainment, which gives much of our idols and role models, body image disorders can be especially noticeable.

Her character in "Harry Potter and the Prisoner of Azkaban" and as a governess with scary features in "Nanny McPhee" appear to revel in roles with odd looks, such as certain exceptionally talented actors like Emma Thompson.

"She appears with very short hair, dressing" mannishly "in her film Carrington (1995), and Thompson said she didn't experience any lack of femininity dressing that way, but rather" lots of liberation, total liberation. I shaved my head, wearing tiny wrap glasses and butch overalls when I went to college because I didn't want to be stuck in femininity.

The "trap may harm many talented actors." "Katherine Heigl [Grey's Anatomy TV series] says she is, *"thankful people think I'm pretty or attractive because I imagine it's better than the alternative. Still, I'm trying to battle it a little because it's not what people see me as. And one day, I'd love to be in a place where I could pick apart to highlight my talent versus just my bra size"*.

But when casting lead characters, many film and television executives don't see anything about the thin, glamorous blonde stereotype.

In a recent LA Times interview, Toni Collette ["Muriel's Wedding" and "The Sixth Sense"] said she doesn't *"understand that you have to look like a model to be a good actress. This would sound not very respectful, but there is a uniform of being you are supposed to aspire to for female actors. There's this latest crop of younger women who all look the same: the same rail-thin body, the same blond hair — the same rail-thin body, the same blond hair."*

Not that all of us do not admire thin blond women, particularly those with creativity, depth, and enthusiasm. Luckily, there are women of all body types in film and television. Though not nearly necessary.

The responsibility of casting directors and actors, as well as producers, might be that. In a 2003 interview, Emily Procter, who played Detective Calleigh Duquesne on the CSI: Miami TV series, and Ainsley Hayes on The West Wing, said, *"It's so cool to have people make you do smart stuff after ten years as a blonde actress in Hollywood."*

In fashion, the light-skinned cheerleader looks too prevalent, and cosmetic advertising, movies, and television must constantly influence the sense of what body standards are attractive for girls and women [and even men].

Many ten-year-old's dread being overweight, and half of 9 and 10-year-old girls feel better for themselves while they are on a diet, according to the Eating Disorder Referral Organization[EDReferral.com]. "Over 90 % of women recently polled on a college campus sought to regulate their weight by dieting and 35% of improvement to obsessive dieting from" average dieters.

But even without an eating disorder, many talented women and more and more men spend a lot of time and money on changing their appearance: around $124 billion on obesity-related drug services and $1.8 billion on diet books, almost 12 million surgical operations were conducted in 2004.

Body image problems can be challenging for all adolescents, especially specifically for gifted and highly sensitive individuals. In an essay, Annette Revel Sheely, M.A., a counselor for the Talented and Artistic at the Rocky Mountain Academy, states that highly gifted individuals "tend towards a more androgynous style. As children, gifted girls and boys are more similar to each other than their non-gifted, same-gender counterparts."

But in puberty, this can become a major concern, and she notes: "As gender stereotypes rise in social importance, androgynous, extremely intelligent youth are frequently bullied in school because they do not fit neatly into our culture's gender expectations."

According to the sometimes unreasonable expectations promoted in films and magazines, another basis for abuse and pessimistic behavior is being overweight. According to some sources, the average woman is 5'4 "tall and weighs 140, but the average American model is 5'11" and weighs 117. The bulk of mainstream designers are shorter than 98% of American females.

"Psychotherapist Susie Orbach [author of the book Obesity Is a Feminist Issue] remarks in a Ms. magazine article [The Dialectic of Weight, by Catherine Orenstein]," How many hours are spent by accomplished, strong, intellectually interested women being terrified by food, then decorating or denigrating their bodies? Is the gym just about health?

So, the question is, how much of your time, financial and energy capital do you put into improving your body image, beyond just remaining safe and fairly attractive? Perhaps you should use more of those opportunities to grow your artistic talents.

Children And Body Image

I've been jokingly told that the land of beautiful people in Hollywood. We have to turn from right to left to realize that the picture of the body plays a crucial part in the culture and daily life. This is even more so in the entertainment field. What are we teaching children proper nutrition? How can we teach them to have a good self-image without regularly copying the negative extremes that might be surrounding them? With little girls trying to imitate their favorite pop stars and models, it isn't going to be easy—boys, too, trousers on the deck, and all of that.

This training and instruction must start at home, as with all behavioral patterns. An adult would never try to restrict the caloric intake of an infant to help them lose weight. Children have growth cycles and spurts they can go through. A child will suffer both behavioral and physical health difficulties by reducing nutrients in their diet. You are off to a good start if you have set up a balanced meal and snack routine at home. Attach the motions and any exercise.

It can't be helped that our kids outside the home are going to be highly affected. TV, books, video games, and peers, all of which appear to have a larger effect on your kids than you do. I couldn't tell you how many times my children have said to me, "Mom's old-fashioned; she doesn't get it." Before I reach 50, you couldn't imagine how I feel right now! Kids would aspire to be like their favorite idols, whether in the film industry or not. For years, it has been like this, and its prospects of improving very soon are dim. In this sector, parents need to watch their kids, much like every other boy.

An eating disorder and depression may be demonstrated by signs of unhealthy eating behaviors, medications, low grades, and behavioral difficulties. Issues such as these can impact any child, not just those in the industry concerned. It's wrong to mark children who participate in television as the ones who suffer more from disorders; you learn more of it when these children are in the public domain.

Raising a child needs a village. Having learned this a million times at least, I don't feel afraid to tell you that I didn't get it. I felt obligated to look up the statement and see what it was all about. Interestingly enough, it's an ancient proverb from Africa; the approximate period is unclear. Jane Cowen-Fletcher, an artist, wrote a book in 1994 called It Takes a Village. The novel was about a little girl looking for her little brother and finding that he had been taken care of by the village the entire time. This is well and well, and I'm all here to save the world, but the village starts at home when it comes to your kids. They want to pursue the parents of every child regardless of what course of life. They need to take a hands-on approach. Not only concerning diet but in general, all facets of life. It is important to communicate; engagement in the life and career of your child is a must. You will help to prevent certain pitfalls by integrating yourself into the life of your child.

Body Image Impact on Women

Now that the media advertises and encourages a very dangerous pattern of excessive dieting and other poor eating practices for women, it has become evident. Some newspaper outlets placed pictures of skinny emancipated females on their covers. They manipulate the subconscious minds of the masses by doing this. And women want to waste their money on television ads seeking to create this unattainable appearance they continuously see.

Let's answer the following questions to try to solve this problem.

1. What's the picture of a body?
2. What kind of patterns are we now seeing in the advertising industry?
3. How does the media change our understanding of the representation of the body?
4. What would the motives behind this be?
5. What are the ramifications of a pattern of this kind?
6. What are any real tips for enhancing the appearance of your body?

How you view, think, and feel about your body is your body image. On the actual look, this could not affect at all. For example, in Western countries, it is common for women to think they are bigger and fatter than they are. Just one in five women is happy with the weight of their bodies. Their height and form were overestimated by nearly half of all average weight women. A skewed body picture, including dieting or eating disorders, can lead to self-destructive actions. Out of 10 young Australian women, about nine dieted at least once in their lives.

Therefore, the underlying trend in the advertising industry at the moment is to encourage the attractiveness of slender, even skinny, unnatural looking women's bodies.

People of all ages, especially young people, watch magazines, TV, movies, and other media items full of photographs showing thin women's bodies. And the subconscious mind of young women perceives this as a role model to imitate and hope to be like. It does not easily attain this skinny look; it eventually leads to any dieting, excessive exercise, or abnormal eating habits being exercised.

The average model weighed 8% less than the average woman 20 years ago — but today's models weigh 23% less. Advertisers presume slim models sell merchandise. It received a truckload of letters from delighted readers welcoming the change after the Australian magazine New Woman recently featured a photo of a heavy-set model on its cover. Yet, it objected to its sponsors, and the publication resorted to showcasing bone-thin women.

What may be the reason for all of that? Why is this fashion movement taking shape now?

Why are beauty requirements put on women, the bulk of which are larger than all of the models, naturally?

According to some experts, the reasons for this are socioeconomic. The beauty and diet products companies are ensured of growth and income by providing an attractive look that is impossible to obtain and sustain. The nutrition sector alone is estimated to be worth $100 billion (US) a year. This is a lot of money, and it is surely worth their time to continue supporting emancipated women as a rule.

And the ramifications of this pattern are immense. Women who are anxious about their bodies, on the one hand, are more likely to purchase makeup products, new clothing, and diet pills, or other diet supplies.

On the other hand, the study suggests that exposure to photographs of slim, attractive, air-brushed female bodies is associated with depression, loss of self-esteem, and the creation in women and girls of inappropriate eating habits.

Per year, the number of eating disorders such as anorexia and bulimia is growing exponentially. Around 5 percent of women and 1 percent of men are reported to have eating disorders such as anorexia or bulimia, or binge eating at any point in their lives.

And about 15 percent of all young people have eating attitudes and practices severely distorted, which can quickly lead to anorexia or bulimia.

But, without resorting to poor eating habits, what will be any real ideas for how to boost your body image?

The first is to move your focus from gaining weight to only maintaining your wellbeing. Second, it is to concentrate more on your characters' inner beauty, such as improving your self-esteem, self-confidence, and intrinsic strengths.

Get updated by reading about body confidence disorders and books about self-improvement. And if you believe you might be vulnerable to this kind of mistaken assumptions, give yourself a break from women's magazines and mass media ads for a moment.

To sum up, the media has a huge influence on women's self-image, and it may have a detrimental impact on women's physical and emotional health. And the best way to avoid these harmful effects from the ads is to teach people not to judge themselves by the beauty industry's expectations and learn not to equate themselves with cover girls. And it is also important to foster a healthier lifestyle that focuses on inner beauty, such as enhancing self-esteem and self-confidence. Not about being a model-like stick.

Perfectionism & Body Image On College Campuses

Campus Peace has the chance to chat about perfectionism, body image, and the countless number of young women who are suffering from eating disorders today with Courtney E. Martin. Martin is the author of Hungry Daughters: The Terrifying Modern Normalcy of Hating Your Body, the new book Beautiful Children.

Campus Calm: Give us a description of who the Hungry Daughters and the Beautiful Girls are and what they represent?

Courtney: Of most women, the ideal girl is that part. I know there's never enough there. Success is never enough; they are never slim enough; they never pay enough attention. In all facets of our lives, there is this hungry desire for perfectionism. The upside to that is that we're success-oriented. We took the feminist tradition we inherited and did some pretty unbelievable stuff about it.

The downside is the hungry daughter's role, who is the ugly underbelly of all that accomplishment. It produces toxic feelings to aspire for the elusive perfection. The hungry daughter is a fairly wise part of us. Unfortunately, when we have the dichotomy on that perfectionist's voice, we always shut up the hungry daughter in us and stop listening to that. It's the part that says, "I'm tired, slow down." We're becoming these high-achieving, robotic, flawless girls. The perfect girl and the hungry daughter have a great deal to tell us. They end up being in this arm-wrestling instead, and sadly, in the center, the body is the perpetrator.

Campus Calm: You said, "We are a generation of young people who were told we could do something and learned that we had to be everything instead." What does it mean for you to feel like you have to be anything?

Courtney: Perfection was a thing about me that was self-imposed. Some parents press very hard on their children. My parents have not. Yet, they both had very high achievement scores. My mom was doing nine million things in total, sort of her community's core and amazing. I was watching her, and I was motivated by it, which is the positive side. But it also caused me this anxiety of wanting all people to be everything. I wanted to be athletic but still clever, and be cute, of course, and talk to the football team's quarterback. And that is the self-imposed notion of getting everything.

This stems from wealth as well. It's probably still a class issue. I was raised by parents who took me to art classes and paid me to go camping in the summer. All these wonderful things about life were continually introduced to me, and I was assured that I was really special, as so many children from our generation were. The wonderful thing was that so many fantastic possibilities were presented to me, but it also produced this seed of fear that flourished with college admissions.

Too many teenagers believe they have to do something or "I will not go to graduation, and my entire life will be over," if their college resume is not ideal, it just causes such fear.

Campus Calm: Where's the line between wanting perfection and wanting excellence?

Courtney: The question is that. For me, it's something you have to negotiate endlessly. Part of that may be recognizing where a certain level of excellence can be given up. It's a pretty good idea to aspire to be outstanding in the stuff you love when letting go of being outstanding in all.

Campus Calm: You wrote that "Many people have normalized obsessions with food and exercise and socially agree that counting calories or feeling bad for any ice cream cone are just part of becoming a woman." Should we first have to realize that part of the issue resides here until we begin improving anything?

Courtney: I think women ought to make themselves real. If your relationship with food or exercise doesn't make you comfortable, then that is a concern. You're not going to have to be treated or have a drastic eating problem. That's a big challenge if you don't feel like you should make decisions and feel good with them. If enough people did this, just coming to terms with your body image could alter the entire universe.

Campus Calm: Can you talk about why college campuses are so rampant with health and exercise obsessions?

Courtney: First of all, on college campuses, females outnumber males by two million and expand per year. We're the majority of students on campuses, and most people with eating disorders are also the majority. The college was people's first encounter with dieting, becoming obsessed with exercise, or eating oddly, particularly when I was coming of age. You're on your own for the first time, and it's a tough transition. Maybe you're in a new town, and maybe you're homesick, or you've got a horrible roommate. All of it comes together and gives a lot of women a very dangerous time. I met girls in high school who had eating disorders, but it wasn't until college that they truly surrounded me.

Campus Calm: Has your school solved the problem?

Courtney: The knowledge was there. There was a counseling group for eating disorders, but I didn't know anyone who went to it. I think colleges are trying, but I don't think there's anything that can be achieved by a health facility. As compared to it coming from the health center, I think it's all about changing the peer community.

Campus Calm: What are the effects of the eating disorder crisis of our culture?

Courtney: It's something that's gone from one generation to the next. So many of us were watching mothers who either had eating orders unwittingly, or had eating disorders diagnosed, or had their bodies particularly despised.

Then any of these economic consequences are there. Moving to an in-patient eating disorder facility could cost up to $35,000 a month. Once you consider a balanced body mass index, health insurance providers do not protect them. And we've got parents falling into trouble wanting to help their girls out. Not to mention the $30 billion a year diet industry and the $26 billion plastic surgery market.

We then have some very frightening physical effects. A lot of miscarriage, which many people don't know, is a direct product of eating disorders. The more we're concerned with these problems globally, the less we focus our energy on living life and transforming the environment. Based on the amount of energy, time, and enthusiasm we have diverted into this insane fixation on the body, who knows what harm we've sustained.

Campus Calm: In what way is the obesity crisis tied to this?

Courtney: They're the flip sides of the same coin, I guess. I assume it's more about Americans not being able to channel this middle route of eating when we're hungry and stopping when we're finished, eating whole meals, going in ways that make us feel content.

We're a cult of bulimia. All those fictional, artificial, really sweetened foods, we are binging and consuming. On the other side, we punish ourselves and rob ourselves of the pleasure of feeding.

Campus Calm: At the end of the day, it sounds so fucked up if you think, 'I was good today because I ate this and I didn't eat it.'

Courtney: Yeah, it isn't very pleasant. We should go to bed and think, "How present was I today? How kind was I? How many individuals did I speak to or listen to openly?"

Campus Calm: And some talented young people are ambitious.

Courtney: With wonderful principles. Another thing is that. It isn't like any of us are jerks. If you ask these women if they admire kindness or thinness in anyone more, they would say, "Of course, kindness." But they can't give themselves the blessing.

Campus Calm: You wrote: "We all learn the lesson that attractiveness is the universal sign of achievement in this society of women's bodies plastered on advertisements, showing up on computer screens, advertising every possible commodity." How can young women and young men reject what we have been programmed to believe is the supreme model for achievement?

Courtney: I guess it's just a constant struggle for the message to be challenged. Compared to the rest of the world, it takes a lot of perseverance to continuously reiterate your worldview. We can each describe what is beautiful, I guess. I love this exercise of just looking at everyone and seeing what beautiful beings they are on a subway train. There's so much beauty in this world, and it's not a model, slim, one-size-fits-all, platinum blonde gal. The more you can associate yourself with individuals who believe that way and speak that way, the better.

Campus Calm: Will you have to offer suggestions as a young woman wrestles about whether or not to change into a swimming suit this summer and join her peers at the beach?

Courtney: I'm thinking, try to switch the pessimistic voice into a more self-loving voice if you may. So even though you don't feel fabulous, say something like, "Okay, today sort of hurts. I don't feel amazing, but I still know that I'm a wonderful person, and I don't want to miss experiences when I have a rough day for my body. Tomorrow would be better; I need to ride surge today."

It's about letting go a little bit and not having to push yourself to feel perfect for your body when it becomes part of perfectionism. It's about accepting where you are and not wanting self-critical things to deter you from living your life.

Love Your Body Today

Why is it that you enjoy your body? Do you love your body because it houses your glorious soul, as Beth said above? Do you enjoy your body because it helps you feel with all of your senses the richness of life? Do you value your body because it makes it possible for you to build content, hug others, and experience the pleasure of movement? I'm not telling you if you enjoy your body, but I'm telling you why you enjoy it. With the why not the if-to get you to step your mind in that direction instantly, I want to continue the talk about enjoying your body. Girls, women-perhaps you, the reader — have wasted way too many precious moments of life condemning and attempting to improve your body instead of enjoying and embracing your body's gift!

The societal conditioning around the perfect body for women is the obstacle that most women face while enjoying their bodies. For "The Body Store," the skin and hair care goods business, there was a famous commercial that said, "There are 3 billion people who don't look like supermodels and just eight who do." This commercial illustrated that what is marketed as the perfect, typical body for women is the usual body for just a very limited percentage of women. Yet, in ads, on magazine covers, and in the actresses we see in films and on tv, this image is constantly represented.

It is a misunderstanding of reality that generates a scenario where women feel inferior because since their body does not look like this, there is something wrong with it. Via dieting, cosmetic surgery, and many more ways of attempting to make their bodies look like the ideal allow people to judge and attempt to improve their appearance. This societal conditioning has a very toxic impact on women and girls and is hurtful. It is poisonous because they judge it against the marketed standard, rather than praising and enjoying their distinctive form. According to the Social Problems Study Center, "More than 80 percent of 4th graders have been on a fad diet." It is tragic to see the strain young girls face to start molding their bodies into the standard, rather than using this energy to read, experiment, and be comfortable and content with themselves.

It is important for women and girls to become mindful of this programming and to have the confidence to move out of the dictates of these unreasonable perceptions of the body because of the deep influence of this cultural conditioning. So taking back the ability to determine your beauty is one of the first and most important rules for really enjoying your body.

Tips to help you Love Your Body

1. *Take back the right to characterize the appearance*

Not just bringing it back to the cultural / media meanings, but also from people who have made judgmental assumptions about the body around you in life. These individuals did not see your body's uniqueness because they had adopted the cultural definitions and judged you and potentially your own body by these ideals. Take a moment to close your eyes now and visualize, taking back the ability to describe your own body's attractiveness. Take it back from the cultural meanings and the media-"I would not allow you to describe what my body can look like anymore "in your state of mind. Think back to people who made derogatory remarks about your body; a family member, a sexual partner, or other children while you were young. Tell in your head to them, "I take back the right to describe my body's beauty-your words were lies and untrue-and I don't grant them any power anymore." Feel how amazing it feels to rid all of this negativity and distortion from yourself.

2. *Clear up your derogatory thoughts on your body*

Because of your exposure to the societal conditioning of the perceived perfect female body, you have undoubtedly exercised your body's self-judgment for not conforming to the advertised "perfect." These assumptions and negative perceptions are distortions again and not founded on the reality of your own body's special attractiveness. We all have bodies that are unique and profoundly exquisite in various sizes and shapes.

Let go of your rigid assumptions about how your body should look and start seeing how the very qualities that make you special and attractive are the same qualities that are distinctive about your body. Write down the derogatory messages about the body that you are talking to yourself. To free them from your mind, imagine writing them down. Let both of them out-the most hurtful derogatory ones you can think of. Look at these messages-notice how you'd never dream of telling someone else in your life these things. Look at all these texts and apologize to your body, saying, "I'm so sorry I told you this hurtful stuff-I swear I'm not going to tell you this stuff again, and now I'm going to start loving you." Look at these texts again and release them completely-break up the sheet of paper and throw everything away. To eradicate this negativity, some people like to start a fire outside and burn the piece.

3. *The Pleasure of Feeling Your Body Shift workout*

Eaten-this will come from a source of insecurity to have the energy and continue and regulate and struggle against the body as you workout and remove weight from the body and compensate for calories. Imagine running for the pleasure of pushing your body and a wish for it to be safe to have more energy from an effort to enjoy your body. If they do so from a spirit of pleasure and self-love rather than control and anxiety for their weight, the consumers I work with around this topic appear to be able to sustain an exercise routine.

Note that there are activities you don't do in your life for fear that people will see your body-like swimming, dancing, or some other sport. Remind yourself that no matter the form, you get to do the stuff you love. Let go of what people think of you and keep focused on the fact that you have the right to do what you love.

4. *Recall what the goal of getting a body is*

To truly experience life, to soak it in and enjoy it, your body is yours. To view life with all of your senses, your body is a vessel for you. You can feel a warm breeze on your skin, feel the cold water in the pool as you float, see all the bright colors of the sunset, hear all the elegance of music, hear the sounds of birds and trees moving in the wind, feel the softness of someone's hand, feel the pleasure of dance, taste and love tasty food, express yourself with a smile, tears or laughter. Your body is for you, not for criticism or judgment from anyone. As a truly realized human being with finer, richer attributes than just your presence, you are here not as a showcase for others.

5. *Look at yourself with caring eyes as you look in the mirror*

For certain women, gazing in the mirror transforms into a self-judgment practice. They zero in on all their perceived faults, and with their body or face, what they believe is "false." Again, this unrealistic ideal promoted in the media is the benchmark by which they judge themselves. I have several customers who said they couldn't look in the mirror when they first started working with me, and what they saw were these supposed defects. Instead of gazing at themselves through caring eyes in the mirror, I recommend that they change that.

When you look in the mirror and see a wrinkle that you would usually criticize, look at the wrinkle with respect and kindness, and even see the elegance of that wrinkle, for example. Set a strong aim to see yourself through the love lens — interrupt self-judgment and move on to yourself being caring. Before it becomes a routine, this will be something you need to do, but it will be well worth the effort, and you will start feeling wonderful about yourself.

6. *Have your self-esteem be referenced internally*

Instead of your outward image, let your self-esteem be based on your internal attributes. What are the traits that build you-you? Is it your kindness, your unique imagination, your intellect, your desire to have fun, your experience, your sensitivity, your ability to listen to others, or your caring heart? Dream of the people in your life that you enjoy. You admire them because of who they are — the special soul they are — not because of what they look like. They admire you for who you are, for all the unique things that make up you. That's how they feel about you. Learn to love yourself for your nature — not for the physical manner in which you ride.

7. *Explore the deeper explanation for your appearance/weight preoccupation*

It can sometimes be an escape strategy for larger, more unpleasant emotions when obsessed with their appearance. Check-in with you to see if this could be the case. If things were unbearable for you and out of reach in your youth, you might have learned to rely on your weight as a means to escape the loneliness and helplessness of what was going on around you.

Or maybe today in your life, there is a painful dilemma that you don't dare to confront, like a difficult friendship or lack of meaning in your life. You are diverted from facing these challenges by a curiosity for your looks. If this is the case for you, you need to find therapy for yourself to open up to face these emotions personally. By taking the risk of sharing your emotions with a close friend or engaging with a psychologist who can help you work with these emotions, you can gain this support.

8. *Stop comparing yourself to others*

The rivalry is hurtful to both yourself and your rival. Using this is another way of putting yourself down, not helping you feel stronger, but making you feel bad. Vow not to be interested with the electricity of this nature. Instead, if you see someone who is beautiful instead of contrasting or judging yourself with this other-state instead-"She's beautiful, and so am I. "Celebrate the other as well as yourself. This sounds so much better than comparing yourself to them or being dismissive, you can find.

9. *Usually, you judge one of the areas of your body and take a week to enjoy this part of you truly*

Spend 15 minutes a day looking at this part of your body and finding something to enjoy in it, but better yet, do it all day long. The more difficult it is to do this, the more you will like to do it! I read a book about a woman who did this workout, and a stranger came up to her after a week of doing it and telling her how amazing this part of her body was! When we change our way of thinking ourselves, it changes the way people view us, too. You want to change your self-love in your first intention of completing this test, not to control how people see you. You are always going to be what's most important, as you see.

10. *Decide that you are lovely and practice being lovely*

If you are pretty or not, you get to say. If you have taken your power back to describe yourself, as I said above, then why don't you assert your beauty? "Take a day and chant" I am Beautiful "to yourself. Do stuff that makes you feel lovely-wear something special-you love and feel wonderful in it. Walk like you're stunning. Look in the mirror and say, "I'm beautiful." At first, this may feel uncomfortable, but continue to do so until you begin to believe it. Celebrate who you are and your unique, perfect body. We need people who see and admire their beauty, inspiring other people who are caught in their body's negativity to see that there is another more joyful direction to take — the direction of real self-love!

Embrace And Rejoice In The Way You Look

Our trust level is closely linked to our physical image much of the time. We feel more secure if, visually, we look fine. And sometimes, if we look good, we even feel good. Most don't feel well about themselves, and most people nowadays sink into their lifestyle so that they no longer take well care of their bodies.

Although some are commended for how fine they look, many are often dismissed regardless of the way they look. And it's a fact. Others may embrace you for who you are. But come on, let's be frank, one of the many criteria is when it comes to applying for a work a satisfying personality.

So, let me inquire, are you happy with looking fat? Can you dream about looking beautiful sometimes and feeling good about yourself? You should still improve and be well for yourself! To take care of everything down there, while the mind is put on top of the body. By taking care of your body, you will help to melt away those fats. Weight reduction is pretty critical and challenging. Depending on the body's reaction to it, certain weight reduction strategies are effective, and many are not.

I will point out some weight loss ideas and finally turn the oversized waste into smooth and beautiful abdominals.

You need to know how to discipline yourself first! The first step to completing a goal is self-discipline, and it also involves losing weight.

Second, listen to the desires of the body. Your body may not adhere to the type of life that you live. It does not respond to your diet strategy favorably, do not be afraid to make a shift that fits your body needs.

Third, set a minimum workout time of 10 to 15 minutes; you may also set a diet strategy that is easy to adjust to. You have to participate in gatherings to keep you mentally fit. This will aid you in sweating out the body's poisons.

Fourth, aim to improve your diet's nutrition, it lets you remain satisfied for a longer time, so when the next meal is ready, you won't overeat. Stop cooking and eating unhealthy foods as much as possible. White meat, a note, contains more fat than red meat. You should try several recipes and pick and start losing weight and melting away the fats. Eat at least 5 to 6 small meals a day, with an interval of at least 3 hours, to discourage overeating. By feeding to the cap, this strategy will benefit you.

Finally, when it rehydrates, water is healthy for the body and helps you feel whole, too. So, make it a habit to drink at least six to eight glasses of water a day. And, before a meal, consider drinking at least two glasses of water. It can hold you whole, but you're not going to overeat.

If you added the tips plus DISCIPLINE, the weight reduction you needed would be equal.

So, take care of your life, have fun, and live it. After a week of restraint, handle yourselves. Balance your lifestyle for you to be safer and fuller.

Your reality defines the way you think of yourself!

Why am I saying this? In my own life, from past and current knowledge, I believe that to be real, and I've seen it play out in the lives of countless others.

As Henry Ford says, "You're right if you think you can do something or think you can't." It's just how our subconscious mind functions, too. You know, any idea or experience you have is recognized as a reality by your subconscious mind. Then it continues to look for evidence to justify these "facts." By encouraging you to make decisions that support what you believe, your subconscious mind will generate evidence. Your subconscious will look for the proof needed to conclude that your ideas are possible if you think you should do something. But if you don't believe you should do it, your ego will hang out and even sabotage you to prove you were right in the first place. What you believe, in other words, is what you get.

For life in general, it's the same. The driving force of your life is your perceptions. If you see things as daunting and defeating, you will fail because you have built a pessimistic expectation that blocks all hopeful possibilities. And presume that you understand items that function well and exactly as you intended. Under that scenario, you will find that you have more than enough motivation to continue on the path while enjoying the journey. The negative stumbling blocks will be balanced out of the ambitious goals. There may be obstacles, but when you know you can, you'll conquer them.

What are you saying about yourself, then? And what are your views on the world around you? Dream of what your current life experience is if you are not positive. It's going to be an outstanding hint.

You have been taken to where you are today by the decision you have ever made in life. Just like any decision you make in the future will either keep you here or pass you forward, because an idea or a way of thinking is the foundation of any option and action. Without choosing to, whether knowingly or unintentionally, you can't function. What creates the truth is how you think of yourself and life.

And what if it's not the truth that you ideally want? Adjust it then!

What is Attraction Law?

"We're like magnets; like attracts like. You become what you imagine, and you draw." -The Secret.

Up until this point in time, whatever your life experience is right now is a reflection of all your feelings. The story you share about your life; your physical and financial health; the form, height, and versatility of your body; your working environment; your relationships and how others perceive you; your words and emotions produce your happiness or unhappiness. The universe around you is a representation of your feelings in all of your situations.

What you think you get. So, expect what's best!

Women who embrace and appreciate the age they are

Growing older is one of the greatest worries that women face. It is not so much that they are scared of death, but more of them are afraid of getting older when they grow older. They should buy and do everything they can afford to keep wrinkles and other improvements in the body at bay on the market. They work a bit sometimes and not much at all sometimes. Of course, for as long as you can, there's nothing wrong with wanting to look as fine as you can, but inevitably, aging catches up with all of us, and we have to find ways to come to terms with it learn how to love ourselves.

The ones who are insecure in their skin are some of the most miserable women you could come into. Only feeling bad about their age and being constantly disappointed with their body and face changes will make them look older because they are not comfortable. Whenever anyone on the inside smiles, the smile can also be portrayed on the outside. You may still have all the latest wrinkles you don't care for, but happiness is easier to come by because you have grown to live in harmony with them.

It is a dead-end street to be self-conscious about your age. You will never be able to avoid your true generation, even though you lavish all of your money on cosmetic implants and a lift here and there. Don't you suppose it would be easier only to recognize how old you are and work for what you have naturally? Not all women agree with this, but it appears that many women are learning to accept whatever generation they have become and have learned to make any moment of their lives exclusive to themselves.

In most situations, you are just as old as you sound. If you encourage it to, the way you look has nothing to do with it. Today's wise older women have learned to be proud of the wrinkles that could be disliked by so many other women of the same generation. Strangely, they sound like they have won them, and they are evidence of the life they have lived, both the bad times and the good times. You have the nice laugh lines as well as the wrinkles of worry. Life is too brief to think about how old you get and whether you're looking nice enough to impress other people. It should be all about being happy, about loving what's going on in your life right now, and about being who you have grown into over the years.

Feel Confident With The Body You Have Right Now?

I am now an utterly better person than I was when I was eating compulsively. I went from a person who rejected an invitation to a person who finally wants to hang out again with friends. From a guy who hardly ever smiled to a guy who had my personality back. I fear making fun of me because I was overweight to a person who waves at my age's people. After all, I like myself and don't equate myself to someone else, from a person who would be ashamed to walk next to people my age. From a person who was not interested in making new friends to someone who made wonderful new friendships. From a guy who was unhappy with a person who loves me so much for every part of me.

I learned how strong I am and how focused and concentrated I remain in my true determination to assist those suffering from compulsive feeding. It's not just about me; it's about the lives I should change. They're all about emails showing me what an inspiration I am. It is something I've ever been serious about doing.

It was a very incremental process, but I believe that the way to go is slow and steady. I have built a strong base underneath me, and I can confidently say that compulsive eating never crosses my mind. Ever not. All the time, I get emails from people wondering if I ever eat compulsively or even worry about bingeing. The reaction is no. What used to describe me was compulsive feeding, and I never want to go back there again. I never want to go through the hardships and trying times of my best companion being food.

I feel like I know how non-bingers think about food because, after over eight years of struggling to find a way out, I've entered the group. I get emails from individuals who want to know if I have ever consumed any of the things I used to gorge on. I eat all that I used to gorge on sometimes, except for fast food (I never eat fast food anymore). I say that sometimes, not because I'm scared, I'm going to gorge on that stuff, but because I have a new perspective on my life, and my attitude is completely different. It is only by preference that I do not drink many of my previous compulsive ingredients. Focusing on consuming nutritious meals that can supply my body with nourishment is just my choice. I wouldn't say that I enjoy the way I feel when I eat junk, and I don't buy it for that reason. In my home, it's non-existent and pretty much in my whole life because I never really crave it.

Now, I want you to know that I am not asking you to brag about this. I don't think I'm any better than anyone. I have been where every one of you is right now, and I have a huge amount of appreciation for the diet trials you face. When compulsive eating controls your entire life, it's a tough place to be. So, then, why am I telling you this? I mention this to you, and I want you to know that you have so much to look forward to. For you, there is a whole life out there that you haven't yet seen when you're held back by compulsive feeding. My days are no longer full of darkness; now, my days are lighter than ever, and for both of you, I want that so badly. I'm so curious to see what the other half of life is like for you.

Right now, I want you to think about your life-what you wish you could do but do not do because of compulsive eating? Perhaps it's due to the weight you've acquired over the years by eating compulsively. Or the mere fact that you don't feel well about yourself and you want to hide from the world might be that.

What activities are robbed from you by compulsive eating?

What's this going to deter you from doing?

Aren't you as social as you used to be, though?

Are you isolating yourselves?

What were the priorities that compulsive eating took away from you?

Finally, what are you going to do for yourself today, the most important topic of all?

For now, try to rely on yourself. You are also persevering and trying not to let any losses hold you down, even though you have chosen a long path that will have many challenges. You are, most certainly, tougher on yourself than anyone else is. Why not begin to thank yourself for what you've done? So what if yesterday you had a hard day? Are you going to focus on it, or are you going to pick yourself up and start fighting for what you want?

Do something positive about yourself today. Anything that indicates that you are going to try to accept yourself further. What about buying a new wardrobe so that your existing outfits don't need to make you feel frumpy? Buy one for yourself that you feel comfortable wearing. You would prefer to do a spontaneous act of kindness, which always makes me feel good about myself. Another choice is to have a massage, a shave, a manicure, or a pedicure to pamper yourself. If you've been seeing your friends for a while now, why not get some friends together and catch up? By doing something for you that would put a smile on your face, do yourself a favor.

In general, I found my whole perspective on life seemed healthier after I got out of my bubble and started doing stuff that made me feel good about myself. I have not thought about what was wrong with me. I didn't beat myself up for something that I wasn't able to improve. I was more hopeful instead and felt that the struggle to beat compulsive eating was more achievable than ever before. I felt new confidence flowing over me, and I decided to push myself to the edge to see what I could do. Honestly, I realized deep inside me that I was going to beat Compulsive Eating Disorder for the first time in my life. I just had the impression of a stomach ... And my feeling was right because, for almost three years now, I've been binge-free.

There are challenges with everything in life, as you know, but I want you to know that the reward of overcoming compulsive eating outweighs all of the tough times you might face. I can't wait until you impress yourself with items that you didn't think were possible because of compulsive feeding. It's such an awesome experience!

Body Image Special

We are also our very own greatest adversary. More negatively than those around us, we judge ourselves. And nothing is clearer than people who talk about their bodies in a derogatory manner. They live in their bodies and help them glide around this thing called life. So, what if by getting a bad body image, you were able to stop damaging yourself? What will life then be like? I have five steps here to help you learn from now on how to enjoy your body, so we can at least have the chance to find out.

Phase 1:

Choose one body part that you enjoy. It may be any part. A supermodel once said it was so fragile and practical that she cherished her wrist b / c. I've had friends say thighs, not only because they're amazing but also because of those thighs, they run marathons. And you should make a list of five pieces for justice and then pick one. Even to me, it's a toughie. I suppose I've been through a lot, but I've got a lot of favorites. Yet my eyes are the best because they are how I see the world, and people praise me on them all the time.

Phase 2:

Put on an ensemble you look awesome in. And if you don't have one in the wardrobe, go out and pick one up. We are in a slump right now, so you might need to go to a thrift shop or even ask for support from some close friends. Say them you're doing (and get them to join in) a body image makeover experiment. Spend 30 minutes in front of the mirror until you are in the dress. Making yourself like going to a really important case, enjoy the time it takes to get ready, and pay attention to things you like. Yeah, it might be a super curvy waist for you!! Note the things that are unpleasant to turn them around.

Phase 3:

Create a little journal/list and write down five things you find about your body that you like every morning. Whether there's no- stretch for you. Using material that other people care about. But even though it is anything like the shoulder blades, enjoy them.

Phase 4:

Go through a few magazines (good or fashion magazines are celebrity journals). Although I'm a big fan of the media cull, you need to cut out various kinds of bodies this time. I want you to see as many of them cut out as you can find. Big tits, smaller tits, no waist, super short (Beyonce) waist. Big nose, small nose, long hair, short hair, black skin, and light skin. You are using a glue stick to put any of these cutouts on the poster board. Fill the board with the poster. Stand before it now, and remember how many Distinct entities there are. Various shapes with various types. What type does your body have? Is it close or not to those you see? You don't need it to be stick thin like Nicole Richie's if you have a curvy body like Kim Kardashian. Remember how special your body is. Add more pictures of body shapes that are more like yours, slowly-not Smaller for you to aim for, but I think a big ass is okay like yeah. Look at the way that J.Lo functions.

Phase 5:

Avoid criticizing people on their bodies and join with peers or openly in this. You will stop judging yourself the more you stop judging others. Please stand up, yes, and be proud that this body is yours, and you deserve it. Since this, everything that is gravy.

Learn To Love Your Body!

It's funny how we sometimes recall odd things that people in life have said to us. One of the memories I have is sitting with my grandmother on a bench in a public location. She was showing me the fun of sitting and seeing people. "Short ones, tall ones, fat ones, slim ones, black ones, white ones. Just listen." These terms have stuck with me for some reason, and I always think about them.

When I spent time walking through the woods last year, I started to think about the woods' scale. Several organisms occur. They are tall, short, round, overweight, elderly, young, dying, and alive. Have they compared themselves with one another? If we sit still and listen, watch and think, we will learn too many lessons from nature. Why is it that people found this desire to compare ourselves to each other? Why can't we all be like leaves, plants, and beasts?

Our body is a vessel for even greater 'something.' Do you love your body and value it, regardless of its height, color, age, or whatever? When she talks to various women about their bodies, I loved listening to Eve Ensler's book The Healthy Body. There is an African woman with whom Eve speaks about her 'body.' I love the African woman's reaction to her. She was a smart lady. If you don't mind listening straight forward, by the way, it's worth listening to the hardcore language.

There is a picture of 'great' fixed in our consciousness as we look at most magazines, commercials, actors, television, or culture. Why are we going to support this? In our way, we are Both perfect. All of us are special because if we weren't, then we wouldn't be our own. The world is one with imagination. So, why on earth should we be people who are cookie-cutters?

Diversity is lovely. Small, tall, overweight, skinny, African, Asian, Indian, European, young, elderly, bad, wealthy, dressed in style or not ... enjoy and honor the body. Suppose marks must be used. In certain ways, you can respect your body because only you know what is best. Enable you to be yourself. Stuff still shifts. And when we change the seasons, so do we.

No matter where we are in the course of who we are, we should love and value our bodies. Here are a few ways for you to get started:

In nature, enjoy some calm and contemplative time.

Look and focus on the trees or plants.

Nourish your whole body with fruit.

You don't equate yourself with someone.

To be true to yourself and not to care about what people are saying.

I'm just dressing up in your way.

Grey hair is lovely — go natural and let your experience shine.

Enjoy a long hot bath, some candles, and herbal tea.

Enjoy a massage or special therapy.

When standing in front of the mirror, recognize and talk to the body about everything beautiful without judgment.

To express gratitude, adorn a certain part of your body that you have not honored with jewelry, body jewelry, clothes, or a special gift.

Adjust your convictions.

Think on your own.

Help businesses that respect diversity. If it's age, race, height, or what?

Get out of an intimate relationship with yourself.

Do something you've always been involved in.

In ways that you nourish your body, be imaginative. People are watching as you step down the highway, or maybe you can look at the elegance at work that goes even deeper. May you be an inspiration and an encourager to others by loving and protecting the body? To the body that moves through the path of creation, have thanks.

Can we dwell on the terms 'for some cause' that stick with us over the years and give thanks? If it's a small one, a big one, a fat one, a slim one, a black one, a white one ... no matter what, love and honor your body.

Ways to enjoy and get in shape for your body

The pressure is in high gear to get fit and safe. People are ready to learn the right ways to put themselves on the easy road to happiness and wellbeing.

However, one error that many individuals make is neglecting their bodies' fundamental needs as they pursue their search for a flawless physique. During your path to greater health, you have to resolve your physical, mental, and spiritual needs. That's why you must learn to love your body and to enjoy the joy of being YOU!

Loving your body means that the beauty of the moment can be welcomed, and you can understand who and where you are right now. When you can do this, it will help you achieve fulfillment and enjoyment at any level of your exercise routine.

Here are five ways to enjoy your body and move on the journey to healthier health now:

Lower The Tension Boom

One of the greatest enemies of the mind and body is tension. If you maintain elevated tension levels, your exercise and wellness regimen can be sabotaged, no matter how intensively you work out. Stress mitigation is a vital factor that can prove what you feel for the body. Yoga and meditation are two approaches that have been considered useful for many individuals to counter tension. As long as it is an exercise that makes you comfortable and eases the overwhelming pressures on your mind and body, it does not matter what you chose to remove the stressors of your life.

Better Alimentation

Many times, you have learned this, but it still needs repeating. How your body looks, sounds, and reacts has a lot to do with your food choices. It would help if you learned to make smart choices on the things you are going to consume. Power your body with fruits and the freshest vegetables. Toss out the over-processed junk snacks and frozen bags of meals and learn the pleasure of eating well to prove that you care about your body.

Act using Weights to exercise

Exercise when it comes to enjoying the body is all-important. Aerobic and anaerobic exercises can require a full workout schedule. If you have integrated weights into your daily workout regimen, it will help. Not only does it work with weights to burn fat to help you get heavier, but it also creates bone resilience, which is a huge advantage for the body.

Grab the time for you

A little self-pampering, not a privilege, is a requirement. You ought to put aside an hour or two at least once a week to indulge yourself. The best way to unwind is a relaxing relaxation with hot stones. It will rejuvenate your tense muscles and aching hips, and you will find that you suddenly have a "new lease on life." It's always nice to have a luxurious spa day at a nearby salon, but you can just as comfortably immerse yourself in a tub of hot water at home. Set the atmosphere with candles, roses, and natural oils, and the good impact this calming period has on the mind and body can soon be seen.

Move along with the River

Maybe by being tuned to the messages it sends, the only way you can show your body how much you love it is. If you listened to these signs before starting some workout or fitness regimen, it would help. Don't expect more than you can give from your body. Pace yourself as you grow your strength and agility. Don't equate yourself with someone because it is special to your body. Know that it is a marathon work in progress to get in shape, and it is not a 24-hour sprint. Take stuff at a decent speed and encourage the flow to go with you. If you work for your body instead of against it, will you cross the finish line in top condition, and is this not a real act of love?

Tips for Boosting Self Confidence

Have you ever been around someone with amazing faith in yourself? If so, you're likely to recall the person well.

Confident persons are unforgettable. Charisma and a certain joie de vivre exude them. Their enthusiasm is infectious, and it's empowering just being around them. They take and put the almost unimaginable within reach. And they're making it all look simple.

Have you ever asked how optimistic individuals get that way? Do you ever secretly wish you could lock up their self-confidence?

Data indicates that optimistic people are more appealing to their colleagues; they have better careers, are healthier, and are more effective than their less optimistic colleagues.

Were they born like that? Contrary to common opinion, the answer is "no." Creation of the trust is a practice, like any other aspect of existence. Motivational speaker Tony Robbins says, while he makes it look simple, he prepares his seminars for hours and cites his everyday routines as the best predictor of his performance.

Take Tony's advice and make it a non-negotiable part of your life to build faith. Here is a list of my eight favorite activities that raise morale. Beginning today, bring one or more to work in your life, and watch your confidence rise significantly.

1. Do function on mirrors. Look at yourself in the mirror every morning and say, "I love you." This might sound weird at first, but keep it going. Expand on this for a few days and say, "I appreciate you. I accept you. You are lovely." Continue this every day, and every day you will feel your morale growing.

2. Using assertions. Do these alone, or add them for an additional boost to your morning mirror job. Examples of trust affirmations include things such as, "I am beautiful, and everybody loves me," "I am relaxed and confident in social settings," and "I am relaxed with groups of strangers." Two years ago, every morning, I began doing 85 affirmations in front of the mirror. Thirteen minutes of my day is the best use

of time. As of two years ago, my faith and the woman I am today are almost unrecognizable.

3. Only imagine. Take time to close your eyes and imagine yourself as calm and at home every day. Get into this process in-depth and imagine and experience what it would experience like if you were every day fully optimistic and self-assured. Imagine yourself going into the gym or shop with your head raised and your shoulders back, keeping contact with your eyes and waving at anyone you step by.

4. Move beyond your comfort zone by yourself. Stick to at least once a week doing something different. Start tiny and continue to work upwards. You'll be surprised at how easily you use this approach to develop. Commit yourself to smile at a stranger this week, for example. Stick to doing it twice a week, then three days a week, until you feel good doing this. At first, it may seem uncomfortable, but when the person on the receiving end of your smile smiles back, you'll light up! Inside and out, you'll still feel great.

5. Practice radical self-love and recognition of oneself. Every day and in every way, you can take care of yourself. Start by making a list of the things your perfect friend will do for you and lavish you with affection if you have trouble investing time in yourself, and then do them for yourself. E.g., once a week, you might give yourself roses, write yourself affirmation and love notes, take better care of your body by exercising and eating well, spend time doing stuff you love, and take time every day to relax. It is nurturing to practice progressive self-love and contributes to self-confidence.

6. Enter Toastmasters or any party that speaks in public. Seventy-five percent of Americans are terrified of public speaking, but one of the best ways to create confidence is to be in front of an audience, and it requires preparation. In a

healthy, welcoming atmosphere, Toastmasters, a 90-year-old multinational group of 366,000 clubs worldwide, is an ideal way to develop social and speech skills. Each participant goes on a 10-speech track, and each participant knows what it felt like to make the first speech. In only six short months, attending Toastmasters has directly helped me go from being afraid of public speaking to feeling positive and enjoying public speaking. While there is a charge for Toastmasters to join, it is typically nominal. Many clubs encourage visitors to attend for free several times.

7. Fake it until it's over. To behave that way, you don't have to be optimistic. Don't you like me? Try it for yourself; strike a "power pose" the next time you feel self-conscious: push your head back, stand up straight and smile. The study reveals that keeping such a posture for 2 minutes tells the brain to feel confident and contributes to empowerment feelings. Find out all about hitting power poses in the interesting Ted Talk from Amy Cuddy.

8. Add SEEs into your everyday life-Self Esteem-Enhancing operations. Practice practices that develop their self-esteem are one thing highly optimistic individuals do daily. In my forthcoming novel, Uplift: Incredibly Strong Practices to Overcome Depression and Raise Satisfaction in 8 Weeks, SEEs can be as easy as arranging and attending fitness appointments such as the doctor and dentist, investing in good habits such as exercise and meditation, or deciding not to engage in your head's critical voice. When they are attainable and require a stretch of the comfort zone, SEEs gain individuals more. Make the idea of SEEs go forward by monitoring them in a log every day. Seeing a list of things you have done every day about yourself brings up self-worth and optimism, good everyday routines, contributing to better fitness and satisfaction.

There you have it: 8 of my favorite self-confidence-boosting tricks. What are you going to try today?

Learning To Love Your Unique Body

Teenagers do crack me up occasionally. They go about spouting platitudes that they want to be recognizable, distinct, their own man or woman-and then dress like their friends, do their hair the same way they do their friends, imitate the same mannerisms they do, listen to the same music, pick up the local slang, accept the trendy color coordination, and show the same attitudes as their friends. In effect, in their search for individuality, they become carbon copies of each other.

The fact is, God made us all special individually. That does not indicate that, beyond that individuality, we are mature. Someone with a quick fuse can't simply say, "That's the way I am." Do you blame your temper on God? That could be an informative conversation. No, our personality and beauty arise from personal interactions that are viewed from a unique perspective that, along with the abilities and shortcomings of the body God created for us, makes us different.

And it's not anything to be embarrassed about. Look, I'm tall, skinny, and I have a long nose ('beak' with that wry sense of humor for those of you). I'm never going to be Mr. Universe (thank God), never win fame competitions, never have fans chasing after me with crazy eyes and cameras clicking away to catch me eating with my mouth open, raving, drooling, lunatic, yelling! How completely stressful, I'm sure.

I'm loving being myself. I know I'm going to change. I think I've got plenty of space to expand. But, I've stopped thinking for a long time about whether people like me or not. I don't prioritize being famous in life, but rather to please God and live for the reason I believe that God made me.

This grants me immense liberty. I don't believe that strangers are mocking me, nor do I think people are out to get me. When I hear that someone meant to injure me with a specific remark, one that I laughed off as a very good, albeit harmless, teasing insult, it always comes as a total surprise.

No matter if others think I have chicken wings, I flaunt my skinniness — I delight in how God made me. And I never wish I was or had anyone else, and that's the way it looks. Besides, he probably needs to be different too, so and so. How nonsensical! Wishing to be like someone who needs to be like someone else, who may want to be like you. Life is fraught with irony. And I love to be conscious of it, even of myself.

Any of you read these magazines in Hollywood and marvel at the sculptured looks of the men and women in them. You wish you had that look. You let Hollywood, for you, describe perfection. Have you ever thought that a significant part of their body would never rot until these individuals die? The way is so much plastic! Enjoy yourself being who you are. Avoid pretending to be another guy.

A happy individual is a person who has the power to laugh at themselves. Don't think about being self-conscious, looking at you, making fun of you, or smiling at you. And you join right in if you've laughed at! There is no liberation from the preconceptions, such as liberty.

And what if my hair gets grey prematurely? It's only one more thing to joke at, flaunt, and pretend that means I have a certain degree of intelligence. I should claim respect for myself, can't I? Maybe. Maybe. I assume it says so in the Scriptures. Somewhere. Somewhere. Probably.

Oh, see? You have extraordinary freedom when you appreciate who you are, accept that you can evolve and change, but are content with who God made you. Being with people and living by yourself makes life fun. All is something to worry about anyway.

Learning to Love Your Body

We are bombarded every day with pictures of models with flawless bodies. It may not be ideal for our self-esteem. When we are continually compared to these unreal, flawless bodies, how do we learn to value our bodies? Oh, or, to start with, don't care about what people say. Getting a good body that is perfect for you is the important thing to consider.

It would be best if you worked out first. Research has shown that doing daily exercise will improve your self-esteem. Isn't it brilliant? Not only are you going to have a better trimmer body, but you are still going to feel fantastic about yourself. So, get your calories out and workout and burn them. You don't need to go to the gym; you can do it at home, work, or outside.

We are all overwhelmed by these photographs of models with so-called ideal bodies, as stated earlier. Okay, guess what? Such a thing doesn't happen! Both of us deserve to get a body we're safe with. Respect the shape of your body and work on ways to be better, and that's the only way to learn and love yourself.

The decision is in the hands of you. Forgive me for having said that. You can tell you're glad that you're overweight and that you can recognize yourself as a fat guy. But are you able? Only honestly? All the time, do you want to feel unfit, unsafe, and sluggish? So, look at the pros and cons, and you'll find that the best decision is still to get fit and safe.

Again, and I can't emphasize this enough, be true to yourself at all times. To be special, you don't need to be like those supermodels. With your positive characteristics, you are a special person. So, work on that, and then you can find that the better you are, the happier you are going to be.

You will find that you are happy about yourself until you learn to respect your body, and now you live your life with a more optimistic outlook. And is that not what we can all aim for? So, learn to embrace your type of body, get daily exercise, and follow a balanced diet, and you'll find that your quality of life is significantly improved.

Here's How You Really Can Learn to Love Your Body

Is it possible to learn to love the body? Each decade brings fresh and unforeseen changes as the years go by. You are passing from puberty to young adulthood and adding weight suddenly. You may undergo the reshaping of your body because of pregnancy if you are a woman. You will finally get into the consequences of age, like wrinkles and the pull of gravity, if you are eager and lucky. Your body will experience tension, sorrow, grief, disappointment, and other feelings throughout your lifetime. You may bear the scars of sickness, sickness, or injuries. Sometimes, the body may be influenced by the effects of a sedentary lifestyle, emotional eating, dieting, or inadequate nutrition. Is it possible to make up with all this going on and enjoy your body?

My Body Acceptance Experience

For me, several years back, decades ago, the journey to accepting my body started. One day, nude, I stood in front of a full-length mirror in the closet. Having gathered my confidence to do so, my goal was to look at my entire body and utter three simple words: "I love you." Trembling, I opened my eyes and looked in the mirror at the portrait. What was the image that mirrored me? As if in a foreign tongue, the three words, "I love you," sounded out in my mouth. What came next was surprising. From within my heart, a bellow of laughter erupted that took me totally by surprise. So spontaneously, the laugh released itself that it took me a moment to decide what had just happened. I was laughing at my statement's total absurdity. As the realization of this reality flooded into my consciousness so abruptly and spontaneously, I collapsed to the carpeted floor, nude, bringing tears from the depths of my despair. I understood my self-disapproval at that time.

So started a journey of awareness and self-compassion, which continues to this day in new and wondrous ways. This self-love path is the eternal unfolding of my holy soul to establish a union in this body and on this planet with the physical self that I am. I am becoming harmonious on earth, slowly yet with visible steadiness.

You have a body, and it's intimate and dynamic in your relationship with it. If you are dissatisfied with your body at the moment, you have the potential to turn your relationship between body and appearance into something perfect, peaceful, and satisfying. You will also learn to build a relationship with your beautiful body, even though there are aspects of your body that you would like to change. Your body doesn't like being an entity ordered or punished for your miserable existence by your vital orders. Your body is the house you live in on Earth for your whole journey. Realizing this symbiosis and trying to create peace is up to you.

Unusually, being happy with your body is something that comes naturally. You can, therefore, shed light on the journey towards greater self-love and acceptance of the body. To continue your trip to love the body in which you work, use these strong tips!

Call a Truce

How do you unite yourself with your body as a partner? Next, order your body to a truce and plan to embrace everything about your body at this point. The way they are, things are. That doesn't mean that you can't try to get things improved. It just means that you are still going to be in a fight between yourself and your body before you declare a truce. In a war, you try to avoid what's going on, but you never really fail to move on to something different. You will continue to create a new, more fulfilling friendship between you and your body by calling a truce.

Your Body Reflects Your Thoughts and Beliefs

On the surface, the body represents what you feel about life on the inside. For starters, you might think on the inside that life is not healthy or that there is no chance of ever feeling better. You can experience sorrow, disappointment, rage, anxiety, or hopelessness because of those beliefs. Maybe you consider that you're a poor guy, unworthy and unlovable. Instead, you might consider that you do not dare to be special, inventive, or self-expressive. Such self-limiting convictions are always painful, and sometimes by too much or too little food, drugs, sex, busyness, or other addictions, you have sought to feel better.

Start discovering new principles that include seeing how your body is not your opponent. Your body is not responsible in life for your unhappiness, and it makes no choices for you. It is not to be blamed for those circumstances if the body is overweight, tired, lacking resources, stressed out, or ill. It's just a reflection of your opinions, values, and behavior.

The best news is that your body is yours. If it is currently hanging on to principles of limitation or lack, it is because of such thoughts you have filled it up. You should make your convictions change! It would consent to keep some fresh ideas that you would send to it because it is your body. When you shed some old ideas about life and yourself and put in some fresh, revised, self-supporting ideas, you need to do a bit of housecleaning.

Practice Thoughts That Feel Good

It could well be a method and an endeavor to transform your body into your temple. But it is an endeavor that is worthwhile. Here on earth, you have a right to live your life and feel good. Within your body is the only way that's going to happen. Be bold, then, and call a truce. Life can be as terrific or as bad as you allow it to be. It all depends on the theories that you are practicing. Learn to match the emotions that feel good within your body with thought. Think of thoughts that bring joy. Question yourself sometimes, "Am I practicing ideas that bring me pleasure and trust?" or, "Am I practicing thoughts that bring me pain?"

The body you were born with can be taught to enjoy. Practice the above suggestions and learn to eradicate the bad emotions about the body that you have. You will learn, in time, to enjoy your life!

The Secret Of Self Care

There you are, everywhere you go. There is no escape, the universe is a snapshot of you, and if there is no spark from the view in the mirror, maybe it's time to challenge the underlying assumptions.

It always shocks me that clients don't do the stuff that can carry them to a better state as someone who has interacted extensively on the body as a personal trainer and holistic wellness counselor. When I look a little closer, I see they're still out there searching for what only 'in here' can be found. Your search for satisfaction will undoubtedly take you to an infinite vortex of wanting and a labyrinth of impossible choices. However, you will still search for the next food, gadget, guru, or cure until you nourish the root of your renewal-your being.

The answer to your quest does not lie somewhere out there. Within you, it lives. Your questions' intention dictates the quality of your answers. Why is self-care on the totem pole's bottom? Why is it more important to make money than to build LIFE? What gives life its sense is seeking the expression of what burns the fire in everything you do. The primary food is your raison d'être-what fills your mind, your essence.

"With the complete sense of love, caring, making, and adventuring, we all perform at a small fraction of our abilities to experience life entirely. Consequently, the actualization of our capacity will become our life's most thrilling adventure." Herbert A. Otto.

The best-kept secret-and we all know it-is that self-care is all about love for ourselves. Suppose you feel that anything out there will get you the satisfaction you are in for a rude awakening-earning $1,000,000 a year, meeting a wife, etc.

There's never going to be enough 'out there' to make you feel like 'here' is enough. This isn't the way that it works. What brings outer nourishment is self-nourishment. It's good to look for the indicators that might mean you're off course if it's been a while since you've felt this amount of vibrancy and energy in your everyday life. What are any indications of that?

Life feels bland or boring because you are not completely interested in working or playing.

-To control, you experience chronic stress and compartmentalize stuff

Your relationships lack depth; your career is dull; your body is out of touch.

-You cannot convey your enthusiasm

-Most of you are in a state of doing vs. being

You're busy, but you have no sense of real achievement.

Will the world sound like this? Right now, who are you? Will your job get you excited? Will your experiences cultivate you? Your body, yes, yes?

Remember a moment when you were completely interested in your life and excited about it. Who were you guys? Being Truly Alive is about savoring the here and now's juicy-ness. Life is not a competition for spectators. Every day, many of us make decisions that deaden our perception of life while making choices that make us come alive! What's the remedy?

The decision is the engine of your creation.

Consider that you are energized, conscious, and enjoying something you enjoy while you're Completely Alive. As you explore the diverse substance of your universe, you are truly present, building your life with love and enthusiasm. You are riding the tide of transition, tuning in, assessing, and choosing the next move. Now you're back, totally committed.

How do you help restore your vital self by being Completely Alive? Every week, it will give you resources and support to:

- Accept your intuitive nature and strengthen the relationship between your mind and body
- Identify your minimal convictions and where you stand out.
- Reveal and realign your energy sinks with your intentions
- Establish a spiritual practice that sustains you-design a self-care regimen that addresses your particular needs-
- Defines exercise and activity that playfully feeds the body
- Increase the efficiency of working resources and play with ease and joy
- Tap your love and help you bring it into your everyday life.

It is for YOU to be Completely Alive-who you are, how to nurture yourself, how to bind to your heart, how to turn up in your world as YOU.

Reclaiming happy habits and wellbeing

It was natural that I would be aware of what I consume and that quality goods and healthier decisions would always be a concern when growing up in a household where food had a greater than normal value.

As I get older, it becomes clearer that one of the greatest factors in my attitude, energy levels, and overall satisfaction is my everyday food choices. The vast majority of people in western society have lost contact with the link between what we eat and our state of well-being. The ordinary diet has been disconnected from nature, affected by our societal background, socioeconomic circumstances, and global supply chains.

These days, living on highly processed products, nutritionally empty, and artificially seen as natural, foregoing all the original foods well suited to our dietary needs. It has been convenient for us to access what we consume, whether or not it is healthy for our bodies. All aspects of our life, not least our diet, have been overtaken by the ideology of lust fulfillment. Within this, we all uphold activities that are harmful to our welfare, and we believe this to be our privilege.

It always takes a sort of catastrophe to provoke change or get us to the point where we reconsider what we have already done instinctively, based on the warmth that our food addictions get us. We have a troubling propensity to look for prescription 'solutions' as complications occur, causing a larger chemical overload for our bloodstream and only offering immediate relief.

The best news is that straightforward changes to our dietary patterns can achieve more successful and long-lasting effects. A very intuitive method can be balanced eating, which is the most normal activity in the universe.

It is not appropriate to underestimate the impact of dieting on health and satisfaction. It was inevitable in the past that we would eat seasonal fruits, grains and vegetables, and home-raised meats. In general, what was available to us was new and un-processed, local. We should re-examine our behaviors and take our wellbeing in hand, right now, applying the rationale of those simple concepts.

We are likely to see immediate changes in all aspects of our lives by providing us with better goods (organic, if appropriate, when artificial fertilizers and chemicals end up in our bloodstream), eliminating heavily refined ingredients, and growing fresh fruit and vegetable consumption.

I need pleasurable substitutes to supplement my excessive indulgences as a gourmand or someone who finds immense delight in feelings of taste. I have been greatly inspired by people, especially in the raw food movement, who have devoted time and passion for finding wonderful techniques and recipes.

If you know how gorgeous you are?

Women enjoy complaining about their failures. You love to chat about how 'tall' your thighs or your ass are, how twisted your smile is, or how beyond recognition your midsection has grown. And one thing is for certain this is a half-full glass way of looking at life that can certainly keep you small and keep you feeling like you're never going to be beautiful.

Want a trick to know? It's not your body that you ought to alter, but your attitude, while your opinion is important. YES! YES! It will change how you feel about yourself by actually changing how you think about yourself. Your thoughts drive you to helpful acts that will make you appear amazing—and looking fantastic leads to feeling confident, sexy, and relentless!

Thoughts= Sentiments= Actions= Results

It can be as quick to move your self-image as to change your emphasis. Your motivation is weaker, your outlook is cynical, and you are unable to see your real beauty because you dwell on what is missing, comparing yourself to others or what you consider to be your 'flaws.' But it will allow you to feel and look good by shifting your outlook and see what is wonderful, fantastic and fabulous about you!

In the eye of the beholder, perfection is. It is, indeed, the idea of beauty that either limits you or frees you! You will begin to see the beauty that you still possess as you come from a place of wealth and welcome yourself, warts and all. Let's redefine beauty to encourage you to start seeing it for yourself.

Maybe you think I'm nuts, but keep reading ...

See, from experience, I speak. I only focused on what was 'wrong' with me when I was growing up. I wasn't as cute as the supermodels in my Teen magazine, and I was sure as hell wasn't as small. I spent hours in front of the mirror, my curves cursing, and my body berating. Except for helping me concentrate on the bad and keeping me little, it didn't do a whole lot. Over and over and over, I said bad stuff about myself, which kept it at the forefront of my mind, which kept me focused on it, stressed me, and made me feel embarrassed. I have come a long way, and that's what I want for you too!

Beauty is not an exterior or shallow thing; beauty starts inside. Loving and embracing yourself in your skin would liberate you from your limited perceptions that you are not good enough and liberate you to see the unique value you already have, regardless of your height, weight, age, etc.

Gratitude is one of the keys to this. The best way to start is to be thankful for what you have a good body, a positive heart, a well-proportioned shape, eyes that can drink in the perfection around you, beautiful hair, etc. It can allow you to see how much you have as you change your mentality from one of lack

(I'm not nice enough ...) to one of plenty (I am grateful ...). This allows you to feel as though you are sufficient, contributing to love and self-acceptance. Being at peace with yourself is where real, natural beauty begins.

Loving yourself on the inside makes loving yourself on the outside so much easier to show yourself in a way that always lets you shine! No more overcompensating for pricey brand names or claiming to be someone you're not! Now is the time to do what's amazing for you. To personalize your appearance and reflect on your stunning features, wear your best colors (eyes, hair). No matter what it is, please wear clothing that's cut for your body style. Wear stuff that lets the soul rise and the heart sing. Wear in such a way as to make you even like YOU!

From the inside out, this helps you to radiate your beauty, telling the world that you know you're perfect. And the cool thing is that what people follow is how your mindset is about yourself. So, deep down in your heart of hearts, when you believe that you are beautiful in your way, others will see it, too! They will sense your peace with yourself and your pleasure, and they will like it too!

Start today, then. Create a list of all your opportunities for thanks and embrace how genuinely lucky you are. Love yourself first, then adorn yourself accordingly. And see how not only your self-image but your whole life can transform this!

Do You Have Real Health?

Most individuals believe that they are healthy because they are not ill. Yet a much more than just 'not getting sick' is true wellbeing. Being well means not only a lack of sickness but also an excess of energy and vigor. Along with mental control, a sharp, quick mind, and the capacity to upset yourself, you have high energy levels and 'get up and go.'

When you have real fitness, your body has the power to fend off infection and sickness. You don't suffer from the preventable 'lifestyle' illnesses that deprive so many people of their wellbeing, such as heart disease, cancer, and diabetes. Your stable body helps you live a long and healthy lifetime, and till the end, you remain fully functioning. After several years of suffering, injury, and ill health, reduced life spans are now normal, sometimes ending.

Being very well, both physically and emotionally, gives you optimum performance.

Yet sometimes people don't have real wellbeing, or maybe they haven't seen it for a long time, because it's hard to do well in life if you don't feel well. It's not comforting when you look at the numbers on ill-health.

There is at least one chronic illness in one out of every two individuals in the country, and many have several diseases. Eight out of ten persons are overweight, and half of them are obese. Even more are weary, listless, and lack the energy or drive to do a great deal to get out of the pit themselves.

Yet, there are only two alternatives. The slippery slope that leads to degeneration will begin to fall, or you can take full responsibility for your health and prosperity. It's all in your possession, and it should be well looked for by you. Who else will, after all?

It should be part of your everyday life to take care of your well-being. The two places where you will make the 'biggest bang for your buck' are your diet and how you workout. These are the two ways in which, if done right, your health status will skyrocket. And if you're 'not well' in these places today, progress would demonstrate major changes in your health and how comfortable you feel.

The fitness program can primarily be weight lifting fitness with some aerobic interval training for completion of the curriculum. Forget about long, boring, repeated walking, jogging, or cycling sports. Being an active individual is awesome, but to restore damaged muscle tissue and regain fitness, a good workout regimen is important.

If you are new to exercising, you need to set up a routine with a health instructor and show you the best exercise technique and how intensely you can execute certain workouts to ensure success.

Your balanced food schedule is the other piece of the puzzle. Try to eat as much natural, organic food as possible. Keep away from packaged foods, which are made of unnatural additives and no health benefits. Look for small meals every 2-3 hours with a source of protein for each. Make up the mix of raw and cooked vegetables from the small lunch. With tons of energy, you can eat about 5-7 small meals per day.

Every day, the little things you do add up to either a good or unhealthy life, and you owe it to yourself to be good, and you have to work at it to make it a success. It is not safe enough to take it for granted when nothing else matters when we lose our fitness.

Various practices for Physical Enhancement

Most healthcare facilities provide health enhancement services to reach a supreme state of well-being and level of operation. It is a fitness program that helps determine your current well-being and then provides you with the appropriate encouragement and guidance to partake in multiple practices to improve well-being and achieve improved health.

Activities for health enhancement that can change your life

In short, fast and easy steps, change your life. To restore health, fitness, and well-being, it is also important to make lifestyle improvements. In respected healthcare centers, there are lifestyle improvement professionals that offer dedicated services for you and your family to help you lead a better, more active lifestyle. Any behaviors that play a major role in changing one's view on life are health and wellness services, weight control, and food control.

What You Will Learn through Health Improvement Programs

- A normal and natural way to reduce weight
- Raising your energy levels
- Managing food allergies
- Alleviating pain and aches without pain medication
- How to incorporate exercise into your day
- How to eat in restaurants and all social situations

To suit your individual needs, the curriculum sessions are organized as a monthly bundle. The kit provides telephone or in-person meetings, strategies for reflection and healing, motivational and mental assistance, functional body exercise, free regular lectures and private workshop invites, and more.

The first step is to decide if the lifestyle improvement program is ideal for you before you agree to engage in the program. It's not easy to pick seasoned and skilled lifestyle enhancement specialists; it takes time and commitment on your part.

The Good Health and Well Being Yoga

I was standing at the bus station the other day when I overheard two people complaining about their weight.

I adjusted my stance to get a clearer perspective of the women without making things too clear, and I confess to listening to their talk. Typically in my behavior, I am not so nosey or noticeable, but their discussion's focus caught my eye. I want to learn what women talk about their bodies and health issues as a yoga instructor. And share what I know to address their questions, if appropriate.

The women were in their late twenties/early thirties from their discussion and observing their body image and regretting the fact that they didn't have time to work out, which is too hard to fit in a gym class, plus they thought it was simply too difficult to eat healthily, considering the high cost of organic fruit and vegetables (compared to normal non-organic products).

And they feel very frustrated, fed up, and demotivated to even hear about changing their lifestyle patterns, all in all.

Do you feel fat, overweight, and flabby?

If this sounds like you and you want to find a way to lose weight fast and comfortably, get fit and feel better about yourself, then take a minute, sit back, and read about some of the advantages of starting yoga.

Three key benefits of Good Fitness and Well Being Yoga

Here are three top reasons why yoga encourages a balanced body, mental health, and mental well-being as a yoga instructor and busy mum.

1. Physical advantages of yoga for positive well-being and positive fitness

An old-time Yogi tells you that you're as young as your spine.

1.1 Yoga activities (known as asanas) concentrate on growing the spine's stability and preserving it.

1.2 The poses are soft and can be changed comfortably to meet both body shapes and fitness levels.

1.3 The soft stretches pass the body in all directions and stretch it. For example, the Cobra Pose offers the back muscles a lovely massage, stretches and extends the ribcage, and alleviates menstrual issues. The Triangle Posture encourages the hips' versatility, stretching the body's sides from your knees to your toes.

1.4 Your balance changes as you get into yoga, as you become healthier and more agile. A good posture gives you a lively, more youthful appearance.

2. Yoga's mental effects for overall health and well being

2.1 The practice of yoga, especially meditation, helps to relax your thoughts and stabilize them.

2.2 You are always at the beck and call of teenagers, work colleagues, and even family members as a working woman or busy mom. The yoga meditation methods allow your mind to calm down, regain space in your brain to become present and more mindful of what is going on in your life. You are more likely to prioritize and reflect on what matters to you while your mind clears.

2.3 Daily meditation exercise encourages the ability to maximize health and well-being.

2.4 Any of my yoga students who have elevated blood pressure or are at risk of coronary heart disease are recommended by their doctors to start yoga as an important means of handling stress.

2.5 A slow method is adapting the diet. The more you get in contact with your food, the more you get aware of what you eat, the more you learn to listen to your food, and when you are finished, stop feeding.

3. The moral effects of Good Health and Well Being Yoga

3.1 Your vitality levels increase as you practice.

3.2 To promote the transfer of energy into the body, yoga asanas, breathing exercises, and meditation all blend. You feel lighter, more cheerful, more at ease. It would help if you regained your life-work-me-time balance from this viewpoint.

3.3 Yoga gives you a clear, healthy, and quick way to regain your life-work rhythm and a deeper life viewpoint.

In Summary,

It's easy for your health to fall low and fed-up. Yet, you can quickly take baby steps to strengthen and endorse positive, healthy behaviors with a little help from your yoga instructor.

How To Attract What You Want Through Self-Love

The most important friendship is the one between you and you.

I sometimes see singles looking outside of themselves as a love coach to get the love, attention, understanding, approval, and comprehension they seek. They say they'll be cherished and lovable if they can have a friendship.

Uh, not really. The fact is, first, what you're after needs to come from inside. You have everything you desire; you might just have lost your connection to it along the way.

Years earlier, when I stuck alone, a friend said to me, "You must first respect yourself." "I'm in love with myself," I thought. I found she was right after a closer analysis. I've lost my link with myself. I was searching for someone to give me something outside of myself that I thought I was losing, to give myself love, to support me, to make me feel like I was loveable, and to do something for me that I didn't do for myself.

To attract YOUR heart's wishes, here are three self-love tips:

1. All starts with you. Whenever you find yourself wanting to get something from outside of you-something that you believe you need or lack, pause and ask: "Am I giving myself these things?"

2. By treating ourselves, we teach others how to treat us. If you don't want to, do you find yourself saying "yes" to something? You might be afraid of what somebody's going to think or afraid you're going to hurt their feelings. Do you have a list of things you want to do for yourself or the objectives you want to achieve, but do you put aside your needs and desires to

assist them if someone needs something from you? It is not self-love to commit to another, which is stronger than the one you have for yourself. This is just one of the ways you prevent yourself from attracting the relationship (or any dream!) you desire and allowing it into your life. You cannot expect someone else to make you a priority if you can't put yourself first.

Growing up, we're taught that it's selfish to take care of ourselves first or think of ourselves first. Yet, do you know they tell you to put your air mask on first when you fly on an airplane before you help others? Is that egotistical? No!-No! It makes you better prepared to help others; you have all the oxygen you need to breathe easier now and help others.

With love and relationships, the same is true. In your relationships, when your focus is self-love, you will experience greater success and deeper intimacy. When you fully have what you are willing to offer, you're best prepared to send to someone.

3. You can't expect someone to love you more than the level of self-love you have. Take this into account: you will attract a connection and love at the level where you love yourself. What I refer to as Buried Values are some of the factors that get in the way of enabling self-love and healthier relationships (and any other goals and aspirations you have for your life). It is a widespread buried conviction to be egoistic. "My needs are bad or wrong," "it's selfish to want things," "what I want doesn't exist," "I have to get my life (body, money issues, home, career, etc.) in order first," are other buried beliefs I often recognize.

You may have some more profoundly buried convictions because you are not aware of them. How do you know? You're not living the desired life and relationships. You could continue to draw the same kind of partner over and over again and don't know why. There's great chemistry, or you meet somebody, but it always fizzles out. About why? Beliefs buried. Your beliefs create your actions and your experiences-whether or not; you are aware of them.

The love and relationship you desire can be yours! You're meant to have love. You're worthy of having what you want. What you want is what exists! What is under the surface and in your subconscious is the only thing in the way.

Quick story: One of my clients has continued to attract men who have not supported her in her job. This made her feel alone and frustrated. She wanted them to understand her and to "get her" for real. What I uncovered intuitively was a buried belief that sharing this part of herself was not safe for the her-the spiritual side of her was a huge part of her business! While it seemed to be the men who were not a fit on the outside, her buried belief attracted these men in. She drew the man of her dreams after we did the healing work, and I gave her practical tools to move forward, and they live together and plan their future. He supports her business fully! Even her own financial goals were broken, and she hit six figures!

Your buried convictions control all!

There are a couple of things you can do if you're able to recognize your buried convictions.

a. Start by paying real attention to the words you are doing to yourself, out loud, and to others. Pay heed to your thoughts. What thoughts on autopilot float through your mind that are negative, disempowering, and don't support what you want? Change them once you have caught on to your thoughts!

b. Build a new cycle of thought to replace something any time you find yourself talking and dreaming, not in line with what you expect for yourself. To transform those old thoughts and beliefs, create an affirmation or a mantra that you repeat.

When you start paying attention to what you say to yourself, you might be a little shocked. Only imagine ~ Can you tell a friend something that you're asking yourself?

With you, it continues.

Ways To Boost Self-Esteem Clothes Through Self-Esteem

"As an extension of the body, clothing can shape the understanding of the body image and works to reinforce or weaken the boundaries of the body image. In defining the self's physical borders, clothing works as a" second skin "(Horn, 1968).

As one grows up, characteristics such as how big they are, what they weigh, race, age, etc., are grouped. Socially, the person has developed their self-perception and level of self-esteem over time. Clothing is an important part of our personality for most of us and has been discovered to give us a feeling of well-being and an added quality of life. It is apparent then that, among other aspects, clothes may have a huge effect on our self-esteem and our sense of acceptance. It seems like the higher one's self-esteem, the less clothing seems to matter, perhaps because they feel they're at their best already, and the clothes they want to wear will still always reflect their mood. Compared to other practices to boost self-esteem, if someone suffers from low self-esteem, promoting body image by wearing the right clothes will have a positive impact on their motivation.

In all walks of life, self-esteem apparel is important, and many different styles fit many different preferences. What is important is that the person feels good and secure in what they wear and in their body shape, so improving one 's confidence is one of the key objectives of improving one's self-esteem. Studies have found that by wearing the correct clothes, more confidence is gained such that you feel comfortable and clothing is a significant feature of personal appearance.

To Give You A Lift, Here Are Some Tips:

- Express yourself through your clothes; the trick is to express confidence by what you wear, including your feet, from head to toe!

  Try to have confidence through your clothes for self-esteem. Once you have the right, what is of paramount importance is how you act and bring yourself out to others. Clothing for self-esteem should assist you in establishing any inner self-worth. The more individuals notice how balanced, optimistic, and interesting you are, the more inclined they are to join you.

- Even though you are not in the mood, try to dress positively to ensure you are pleased with what you wear. You will then draw others in a similar state of mind, and you will raise the mood in trust.
- Know the form of the body. Today, in most sizes, there is gorgeous clothing that matches all body sizes, and choosing the best type that matches you, will have a big effect on your confidence. Only because it's the standard, strive not to squeeze into styles that are too little. If you are confused, on the internet, take advice or check as it could be that you have all along been choosing wrong. Your body

form should still be complimented if you wear the right clothes for self-esteem.

Don't be frightened of experimenting. You might not have it the right first time, but today's jeans are way cheaper than they've ever splashed out on anything new in which you can play. When you feel secure in what you wear inside, you'll come through because no matter what you wear, you will have fun because of trust.

Issues Of Self-Esteem And How To Develop Faith In Yourself

Those children who are inspired to do new things, do not afraid to learn from their errors, and turn around with a more optimistic view of their future have stronger self-esteem than those who are regularly scolded or heavily corrected about things.

Next, let's remember what A Course of Miracles says: "Wouldn't you trade your doubts for the facts if the trade for the appeal was yours?"

It is amazing, so many adults suffer from low self-esteem from daily fear and take it out on their children.

Remember, when things happen like missing a career chance, a marital breakdown, or just the hurdles of life, it's not a fun experience for any of us, and it sometimes results in someone missing some of their self-esteem.

If you're like those who put off taking those steps on the wish of a dream or heart, don't condemn or blame yourself. Start reflecting on the present moment and listening to your heart.

Self-Esteem Boost

First, begin steeping towards a goal with baby steps, but now take action, do not hesitate or put it off.

You will see this alone as a modest achievement, and as your self-esteem begins to grow, you will take greater measures in action faster than you know.

Using the influence of artistic visualization by expanding the mind to begin going in the right direction.

Try to have fun doing it, and maybe the world will see you at the top.

Remember the last time you had low self-esteem when it seemed like something was going against you?

How do you develop a deep trust in yourself, a fundamental belief that lets you survive with far less tension and distress and depressed emotions, and every day you have more joy?

Poor Self-Esteem Support

Let's look at so many otherwise great people who are dealing with poor self-esteem, maybe.

At an early age, people start to grow and build their self-esteem.

There is a more desirable self-esteem perspective for children who are motivated to do their hardest and learn from their failures than others who are continually belittled by things.

Self-esteem can pass through a complete transformation for teenagers.

When their bodies shift, others feel highly odd. Owing to this, they end up not being happy around anyone for a very long time.

However, some end up becoming immensely famous, and they like the publicity. This results in a very positive self-esteem outlook for them. It makes people feel relaxed around them as their reputation increases.

Issues of Self-Esteem

How many grownups suffer from poor self-confidence is surprising. Maybe they still feel this way, or maybe it was because of something in their lives.

In general, losing a career, having a divorce, or just life can lead to losing some of their self-esteem. Many grown-ups are less likely to consider improvements as they get older.

This will lead to them challenging their actions and creating a negative view of themselves.

Growing your self-esteem can be hard; you need to work hard on it, however.

Have you got an ambitious outlook?

The most critical job is to redirect your energies into improving the view of items.

A Course of Miracles allows one to respond, "Will you be isolated and at ease from your identification?"

Instead of thinking over what people don't like about you, think about what you have to offer them.

Then, if you think about how you look, change what you do not want. Start to work out more if you think about your general height.

If you don't think that makes you beautiful, you could cut your hair and style it differently.

To make you feel optimistic!

Stunning On The Outside And Dying On The Inside?

Our bodies are our closest setting, yet many people see their bodies as harmful, gross, shameful, and even ugly. Why is it that so many women don't like their bodies, and what can be done to change their relationship with the one world they're going to bring with them for life?

At a young age, we care about our bodies. Being a child is a state of complete dependence on our caregivers to meet our most important needs. To a child, feeling hunger or cold is a frightening fact, as they sense the sensation of absence or suffering before they begin to know the world as different, without the capacity to know that the sensation is 'out there' and beyond their bodies. The career's attunement to the baby's needs plays a significant role in teaching the infant to experience the environment as dangerous or relaxed (originally 'their' body). Hopefully, an effective and prompt fulfillment of the baby's needs increases confidence and awareness of their bodily needs in the child. This is not always the case, however.

Training from childhood to recognize and embrace our bodies is just part of the struggle to love or loathe our bodies. In school, feedback gives more feedback on our height, stamina, or ability to run and be successful at sports. A stable or dysfunctional relationship with our bodies is established, depending on whether it is positive or bad. Another obstacle comes from the shifting years of puberty, and soon we face the social realm of exclusive beauty. Images from a society where there are certain ways to look attractive are enormously important for women. It thrives in the make-up, dress, and food industries. If this solution is exclusive, i.e., if it is only suitable if a certain mold is installed, it raises fear of being 'less than' or inappropriate and having to modify. Nevertheless, multicultural representations and that highlight individuality of beauty emphasize changing or nurturing ourselves foster even more meaningful relationships with our bodies.

A woman can be 'Stunning on the Outside, but Starving on the Inside' where there is an over-reliance on exterior attractiveness unmatched by a solid, confident internal image of self-worth. She can feel misrepresented and puzzled because she could receive encouraging compliments, desire, or jealousy at the same time as feeling unworthy, ineffective, or even unhappy. Also, social pressures and misconceptions will intensify uncertainty by conforming to socially presented appearance standards, leaving her feeling increasingly isolated and bewildered.

What can a woman do to build a greater sense of self-esteem, approval, and respect for her own body? This can be a daunting and lengthy path, especially where such self-loathing has led to the lack of truly nurturing and treatment of the body. However, initiating a healing process starts by understanding that there is a problem. It is all part of a road to healing. It obtains assistance from others in the form of reading, the internet, and face-to-face community groups that focus on healthy self-development, compassionate therapy, and a willingness and question the norms of society's attractiveness. During this path called Life, transformation starts with a decision to truly understand and enjoy yourself and be your own best friend.

How the media influence your self-esteem and body image

Since I double-majored in Psychology and Journalism, I wrote several study papers before graduating from college. Over several months, a fascinating topic I conducted has to do with "How The Media Can Influence the Self-Esteem and Body Image of An Individual." Social psychologists have also researched the social evidence definition to better understand how self-esteem comes into play. In social facts, if a person exudes an atmosphere of being highly regarded or part of the community by himself and others, that person is more likely to be welcomed and supported by others.

The significance of this research is to provide an insight into the human experience and demonstrate how the media influence individuals in regards to their perception of the body and self-esteem. The research I did could also enable science community experts to create strategies that could help individuals resolve harmful self-perceptions.

Four distinct media forms were presented in the study: radio, Internet, newspaper, and television. A connection between the choice of the advertising medium and body appearance or self-esteem was significant because research in the past has shown that the representations of attractiveness and models depicted by the advertising as the ideal standard are partially responsible for the external demands to retain or appear at a certain weight and have led to eating disorders.

The final point is that recent experiments have tended to link race with poor self-esteem. That claim would suggest that one would be likely to assume that blacks have lower self-esteem than their white counterparts, considering the considerable social standing that black people face, but that is not valid. Blacks display no substantial decline in self-esteem or negative picture of their bodies than their white counterparts, regardless of how negative their environment may be.

A good example is that full-figured women are found attractive and very sexy in some African societies and even in a few ethnic cultures in the West. In comparison, that may not always be the case in non-ethnic societies. A non-ethnic Rubenesque woman may then fill out a questionnaire showing that she is not pleased with her body size or weight, whereas an ethnic woman who is the same size and weight mean that her body is very pleased.

Recently, VH1 aired a Jessica Simpson show in an African village, welcoming her to an African wedding. To look more full-figured, the bride was forced to go to the fattening chamber for eight months and was served a high-calorie diet. Jessica Simpson seemed to be so amused that large women were considered attractive in that particular society. In certain ethnic societies, this is because the figure's fullness is regarded as a symbol of fertility, prosperity, and well-being. Around the same time, in various ethnicities worldwide, thinness in an individual is perceived as a lack of fitness or fertility.

I used two questionnaires in performing this research and using the Rosenberg Scale, one assessed self-esteem, while the other measured body appearance using the Body Image States Scale (BISS). The media was reliant on both variables (body image and self-esteem).

Improving your self-esteem and body confidence can be key to your success.

Your strong self-esteem is your basis for success, and in certain cases, you will feel down, frustrated, inferior, and experience a loss of trust without it. There are several variables, arguments, and lessons on the road to enhancing self-esteem to motivate you. The link between how a person views their body image and how it influences their self-esteem is a significant connection explored here.

Self Worth Building - A Balanced Body Leads To A Healthy Mind.

Floppy loose skin, fat layers are piling up under your jaw and around your butt, love handles, fat folds under your bra line, thighs, hips, roly-poly legs, a fat tummy protruding! There is a link between your body image and self-esteem as to how you perceive yourself, and no matter what compliments other people offer, and if you are disappointed with your image, you will not be able to embrace it ...... a sure sign of low self-esteem.

People come in all shapes and sizes, and it's safe to claim that what you are born with can make you happy. Nevertheless, there is no guideline to suggest that you can change your body image to match up with 'society's norm'... what you need to do to boost your body image and self-esteem is to make changes to the way you think of yourself to make sure you feel safe to so what the more for you if that means exercising. The key thing is that, without the extreme steps of surgery, you feel fine about yourself.

With all that being said, the pressures and pressures of the modern world put people under rising strain, such as making more money, becoming younger, becoming smaller, being a better father, and getting a good job, and so on, means that it is not an easy task to create self-esteem. It will have a good impact on your self-esteem and change how you look, which will finally benefit you with your profession or whichever direction you want to pursue. Some people cope very differently with body image than others, and you can also note that those suffering from physical deformities will have much greater self-esteem than those who do not.

Your decision is how you want to boost your body image. One important point is that you are inspired when you start to experience the advantages, so you will ask why you never started earlier. One major step to feeling better about oneself is just the initial awareness that there is a connection between body image and self-esteem.

Self-Acceptation

Accepting who or what we are is not always easy. Rather than picturing our faults and shortcomings, we all tend to picture ourselves through the eyes of a perfect sort. Of course, the fact is, humans are not fine, even you. Being human means making errors, period! You ought to become diligent about learning from mistakes rather than concentrating on the errors in judgment. Like all animals, by process of trial and error, human beings learn. It is to get hung up on being a human being to be hung up on making a mistake.

So, the first step to self-acceptance is to accept that you are fallible along with everyone else. It can make a real difference to your lifestyle to integrate self-accepting values into your life. On the premise that errors exist but can be rectified, you are advised to remedy past errors or prior deficiencies. Self-acceptance confers a margin of error to you. You may feel suitable and proportionate negative feelings as difficulties arise, and then carry on. It is fair because you are much more likely to fix a dilemma if you don't suffer from emotional pain.

From your talent to your tiny faults, this is what makes you. While you should be serious about being the best you can do, do not take this to mean that you have to take yourself too seriously, but this is not positive for proper mental health.

Their little foibles, idiosyncrasies that label them as unique are a part of what makes people endearing. We find them endearing when we experience this stuff in other people, but offer yourself the benefit of the doubt. After all, no one is flawless, right?

Only because one new idea you tried did not succeed, don't slip into the pit of giving up doing something new.

The fascinating individuals seem to have faced a few challenges to overcome; this is what gives them character. If all of your mistakes and achievements can be seen as important to your character, you are a much better, more robust human.

Do you know how it feels more normal the more you practice something? Oh, it isn't different from practicing a conviction. The more self-acceptance you rehearse, the more you chuckle at the ridiculous things you do, the more adaptive you imagine, the more like that kind of person you become. In your mind, rehearsing a case makes you so much more comfortable to deal with it.

How to Help Your Teen

You will support your daughter to minimize the effect of the media on her body image through:

Have your teen search for role models who are positive for his or her body.

Limit this sort of publicity to your teenage daughter. This does not mean that all teen magazines need to be taken down, to be conscious of which ones consider this teen issue. Before buying a subscription, try them out at the supermarket.

Promote healthier patterns. Help your child work on healthy food and exercise to foster well-being.

It is also necessary to set a successful example by your actions, including having a healthy attitude towards your body image.

Start a program of publicity exposure in her college.

Speak to her on how models' images are changed and airbrushed.

Speak to her about the health hazards of being too thin, and use the internet for informative moments.

Speak about successes rather than beauty.

Teach teenagers to make their bodies recognized. Remind them that people are all different.

Talk to your child's doctor if your child deals with body image disorders that influence self-esteem, temperament, or even eating habits. Your teen might benefit from talking to a specialist in mental health.

Beautiful Body - Tips For Girls

The perception of your body is the mental image you have of your physical presence. Does it sound puzzling? Simply put, when you look at yourself, that's what you see. Your body is shifting, and these new physical changes may make you feel uneasy or ashamed. This could also be the first time you've ever noticed what your body looks like. Know, you are perfect no matter your form or size, and there are things to enjoy about yourself. I take my Ten Commandments to a healthier body image cheat sheet anytime I get one of those "I don't like the way I look for days," and I remember all the things I enjoy about myself.

For a healthier body picture, the Ten Commandments:

1. Thou Shalt Not Blame Yourself: You owe them a lot of energy when you dwell on what you consider are your shortcomings or deficiencies. That gives them control, in turn. Take the energy and place it in your house. Start by writing down one thing a day that you enjoy about yourself.

2. In front of the mirror, Thou Shalt Waste Less Time: It's okay to check yourself out (it's especially a good idea to look in the mirror to make sure your shirt is buttoned right before you go to school). And if you're in love with what you see, go on and keep looking. But if you get self-conscious by looking at your mirror, leave. You've got more interesting stuff to do.

3. Thou Shalt Not Think About Something You Can't Change: There are only a few aspects that you can't change, like your skin color or your height. So, to complain that you're not taller or that your feet are too big is just a waste of time. If you're in charge of what's troubling you, like getting in shape, so start focusing on your target instead of obsessing.

4. If you spend time with good people who care for you and praise you in areas that matter, you will certainly feel great about everything, including your body. Thou Shalt Surround Thyself With Positive People:

5. Thou Shalt Wear Comfortable Clothes: A dress could be the world's hottest style, worn on the red carpet by celebrities. Even then, if it makes you feel uncomfortable, take it off. There are several interesting types to try out, so don't pull yourself into clothing you don't like.

6. Exercise Thou Shall: Rotating your body relieves tension and allows you to become healthier physically. Exercise isn't just about weight reduction; it's all about being healthier. You'll feel better when you get in shape.

7. Thou Shalt Not Measure Thyself A Lot: If the doctor advises that the weight for your height and age is safe, then trust the doctor and go on. It is not as necessary to think about the quantity on the scale to keep a healthier lifestyle.

8. Look at others the way you'd like others to look at you: don't be too dismissive of the presence of others. That means you're not allowed to make fun of individuals for being tall, short, or wearing the last season's shirt. You can skip a lot of cool stuff inside if you judge others by how they look on the outside.

9. Thou Shalt Not Equate Thyself: Maybe your best friend has stunning grey eyes while yours is a rich brown hue. Everyone is unique, and all of the beauty is your own. So size yourself up with your own set of metrics.

Oh. 10. Love Thy Body: Eat well, exercise well, and sleep well enough. It will help you make beautiful music throughout your life if you treat your body like its precious instrument.

Self Image of Women-What Influences?

Women are frequently bombarded with photos of their lives and bodies in fictional newspapers and find themselves contributing to a lifestyle that only affects a small minority. Most women are aware of these hurdles, but they feel the urge to continue to aspire for the "top model" image, and oh ...... 4 'in height.

Our body appearance is influenced by culture. A sturdy woman is known to be fertile in certain cultures and thus revered. In the society of North America, though, there is a fascination with looking slim and fit. Thinness, with popularity and the potential to attract a man, is synonymous with high social status. It has been more strictly defined and restricted to the ideal of white female appearance, making it virtually difficult to be slim enough, athletic enough, or young enough. Society imposes such high and unreasonable expectations that the mold of perfect attractiveness cannot even suit anyone.

The ironic truth for our society is that most women on the covers of high-fashion magazines are white, not without anguish, anger, and/or resentment. The typical white North American woman will never even reach this "ideal" vision of perfection alone of other American cultures. For many women who are undoubtedly undergoing transformations and improvements to their lives for different reasons, these "advertising ideals of appearance" are scarcely received and may continue to attract the scrutiny of how they distort body image.

Numerous body image analysis findings have found that girls from ethnic backgrounds such as African-American and Chinese-American, for example, have higher self-esteem due to their body image compared to women in the same age group as young white American girls. The reasoning was that few girls from these ethnic groups barely related themselves to the photos seen in magazines or on television; these figures were not used as credible role models. The media is doing tremendous harm to the way our young girls see beauty and themselves. Still, the optimistic affirmations of older women who inspire their young lives might reverse this image. Young girls should be offered constructive reinforcement with their body image wherever possible.

Studies carried out by the Melpomene Institute for Women's Wellbeing have also found that women who were 50 years of age and older have to feel underrepresented in the mainstream. A few years ago, in a survey conducted by the institute, it was observed that the proposed weight was 113 lbs and 120-122 lbs for women 19 and older for a woman 5'4 'in height and under 19 years. For women 19 and older. For older women, this is not practical and stable. The issue for mature women is the lack of positive visibility for their age group. Another survey conducted by the Melpomene Institute in 1985 observed the following

A friend wanted to perform a quick survey of my senior women's exercise class, curious to see how accurate these findings were and how far they would be in terms of age and body appearance. This questionnaire was created for women 50 years and older.

A few sample responses from the survey are the following:

"One participant said how she felt unsatisfied that when she was in her 20s-30s, she was underdeveloped relative to other women her age. She also said that what had the most effect on her body image is other women; she continuously compared herself to them. Pleased was the way she described her body view today;" I'm glad I have my fitness and outstanding use of both my limbs and my limbs.

Another female participant said that in her 20s and 30s, she always felt positive about her body; she was always safe and secure in herself and her abilities. She also said she never had bad feelings; she always understood what she wanted and never changed her looks. She said she never did so regularly regarding fitness, but she always wanted to walk and run whenever she liked. My skin is always really beautiful, not just the outer look, and the beauty comes from the inside.

In brief, multiple research findings have found that a woman's opinion about her body image and worth rises with age in general. My brief survey results were no exception; both women said that they became more positive about their bodies as they age. Attractiveness is not only on the outside.

Women come in all shapes and sizes; this should be celebrated. You will only help protect yourself from illnesses and improve your quality of life by keeping a healthier lifestyle with nutrition, exercise, and a balanced diet. Still, it can also make you feel good about yourself.

Here's How To Help Boost Your Teens Self Esteem

Most persons suffer from problems of self-esteem. Problems with esteem also concern adolescents more. Both emotionally and psychologically, they're going through adjustments. This may radically influence what they see themselves and their talents.

Self-esteem is more about how a teen perceives their image. That is how they see themselves as a whole. It may be how they see themselves in events focused on academia, athletics, or success. Doing well can develop self-esteem in these sectors, but that may not be the case. Many teenagers who are excellent in these fields will suffer from self-esteem challenges and are considered good looking by their peers. It is about how they interpret themselves and their achievements.

Support a teen steadily boost his or her self-esteem. In depression or other issues, radical highs and lows may result. Show them that, as a whole, they should feel good about themselves.

Self-esteem struggles may be a result of how adults behave around them—care of your patterns. Your teen sees this as you are actively browsing yourself. They note that it appears that you just point out the negatives. They would emulate this observed conduct. Start by offering yourself a better level of self-esteem.

Show them that not the secret to anything is body picture. They may be immune to a teen who has poor self-esteem due to appearance, weight, or other physical characteristics. The teenage years are a change. In their bodies, they are learning to be relaxed. We live in a culture which, like things to be, endorses appearance and thinness. Teens are grappling with this, including those who suit this mold. Teach youth that what makes the planet a more fun place is the difference. Show us we don't all need to pose like we belong to be beautiful on a magazine cover. From the inside, it comes. This is a challenge that we all need to get acquainted with, not just the youth of today.

Enable them to celebrate their success and forgive their failures. Give them praise if they are doing well on an exam. If they don't do well to convince them that they are OK too, they should excuse themselves and move on. Take into account all sectors, not just educational, athletics, clubs, and other events, no matter how limited they should be included. Encourage them to-do items that are different as well. They're best at trying, even though they fail.

Part of growing up is learning to cope with criticism. Teach your child that it's nice to have positive feedback, but still combine critique with appreciation. A rising youth wants to know that things are well handled for them. This would tend to even out the negativity that they might get.

Be there, most of all, with your teenager. An adolescent with family and friends' affection and support also has higher self-esteem. They are much more secure in other areas if they are protected in this area. For a teenager, understanding that you are unconditionally welcomed does a lot.

Be wary of the symptoms of poor self-esteem in your teens. Depression, eating disorders, alcoholism, or other problems may arise from poor self-esteem. Having yourself conscious will let you know what clinical let will be needed for your teen.

An individual can get far in life by developing a positive sense of self and good self-esteem. It's one of the best resources you can provide to help your teen grow. Lead by example, offer plenty of encouragement, and show them that they are amazing, successful first steps are worthy individuals.

Developing Positive Self-Esteem

Do you find your physical image insecure? When you look at the magazine covers for the new fashion magazine, do you feel out of place? You're not alone if you do.

When it comes to the media's picture of what is pretty and appropriate in terms of scale, form, facial features, or height, many do not exactly stack up. Take heart, however. Just like you are, you're still stunning.

How many fans like yours have just cringed? I'd have to. You hear that all the time from motivational speakers and authors. Just like you are, you are perfect! Just like you are, you are beautiful!

I remember that when I was growing up, I read those notes all the time. Have they helped me? Oh, no. Sadly, I had a mother who liked to remark on my ill-formed characteristics — you know what I mean, don't you? Both of them do and can contribute to it.

It would be tolerable if it was the end of the story, and there are ways that we might get around this issue. This, though, is just the tip of the iceberg.

I know myself because I didn't match up in the eyes of my mother, and because I was taller and chunkier than most other girls around my age, the kids in school made fun of me, and my self-esteem had been struggling for a long time. To avoid breaking myself in two, I had to practice hard, and I was not flawless.

Here are a few things I did when I was tired of constantly hearing something about my form, height, and presence that was insulting.

1. Every morning, I got in the habit of staring at my form in the mirror and smiling at my form and myself, not in ridicule but utter recognition.

2. For each imperfection that I felt I had, I made peace. In those days, I was dismissive of myself. This meant that I said good things about myself or none at all, instead of questioning myself.

3. Through chanting a mantra every morning and trusting the words, I made peace with my imperfections until they were second nature to me. The motto was: You are wonderful in God's eyes in every way.

4. During the day, anytime I found myself thinking negative comments about my appearance or form, I wrote down these remarks in my journal and then substituted them with positive ones. I practiced repeating these positive statements every day for two weeks in front of a mirror.

5. I started journaling about my look regularly. I wrote down all the thoughts I had about myself, and I'm continuing the practice today. This makes me optimistic about myself.

So, follow these approaches and see that you have a more optimistic sense of yourself. If people want to convince you that you're beautiful, it won't work if you don't believe it yourself. You'll be focusing on building healthy self-esteem by implementing these guidelines.

Ten strategies for building Self-Esteem that function

The choice to increase your self-esteem will be a big step in changing your life and earning other people's appreciation. While it's not impossible to build your self-esteem, you do need to know how to do it. To help your self-esteem rise, here are ten ways:

1. Choose your business carefully. Stop persons who are unnecessarily or persistently pessimistic or cynical and prefer others' business with an optimistic and uplifting attitude instead.

2. Get clear on the expectations. You will build confidence and start to feel a lot better about yourself if you set targets and work diligently towards them, making minor milestones along the way to the bigger ones. You improve the chances of completing them by reducing greater targets to a series of smaller steps. Whenever you can take one of the smaller targets off your list, you'll still be able to feel the feeling of success.

3. Think and talk for yourself purposely and confidently. It is easy to be harsh on yourself when things are tough and dwell on your mistakes. However, you can boost your morale and improve your self-esteem if you remind yourself of your talents, successes, and value to your family and friends.

4. Learn to embrace positive feedback and use it. You ought to set constraints on what kind of critique you are going to be affected by. If it is derogatory and an apparent attempt to attack your trust in yourself, redirect it or avoid it. However, you can learn from it and use it for guidance on your professional development path if the critique is positive. In overcoming your shortcomings, helpful criticism will lead you.

Your self-esteem will soar as the flaws vanish, and you become the person that you deserve to be.

5. Be elastic. Be able to get back up again and keep walking if you crash. All struggles in their life at various times; that doesn't mean you're a loser. Decide to trust the best of yourself and your future. Be persistent and recognize that progress is in the future. We would be able to deal with the most daunting of situations provided we preserve our confidence and courage.

6. Don't equate yourself with other persons. At some point in your life, there will still be more successful and less successful individuals than you. You find yourself open to feeling inferior if you equate yourself to others. Instead, measure how far you have come in your own life, not how far you know like you have to go. This attitude to life will strengthen your trust in yourself and boost your overall self-esteem.

7. Don't underestimate yourself. We can end up wallowing in the sense of loss if we do not rebound quickly from our lives' disappointments. It is possible to erode our self-respect, faith, and self-esteem to the point of non-existence. Do the best to defeat pessimistic thoughts and aim to project a positive vision purposefully. The mentality you demonstrate to the world will determine how you are handled and how you are handled will affect how you feel about yourself. You will be more optimistic about yourself if you are handled with dignity. So, try to understand yourself to stop the self-criticism habit.

8. Face up to bullying. Bullies come in any manner, size, and social class. Unfortunately, after we leave kindergarten, they don't vanish. In the office, in our communities, or our peer networks, we will find them. If you are grappling with bullying at some stage, standing up to the bully is crucial. Instead of being violent, practice being assertive and show people how

you want to be handled. Your self-esteem will increase as people regard you with higher respect.

9. Learn and relax for individuals. If you're shy or self-conscious and find it hard to crack the ice around people, you don't know, and your self-esteem may have taken a pounding. Our faith in other people's relationships has a significant effect on how they handle us and how we feel for ourselves—practice beginning discussions with persons that do not understand well or at all. Listen to what they have to say and ask any questions if the conversation gets bogged down. In your body language and your replies, demonstrate your concern. Your self-esteem will grow as you get used to talking to new people, and in social settings, you will become more secure.

10. You need to look your best to perform your best. You would not feel as confident for yourself as if you are well dressed and well-groomed if you sit around in expanded unfashionable wear. Know, the feeling we give other individuals can impact how they treat us and how we feel about ourselves. It is also important to take care of your wellbeing, not only to look healthy but also to feel enthusiastic and optimistic about life. Good self-esteem goes hand and hand with a healthy body.

7 Tips On How To Improve Your Self-Esteem And Attain Higher Goals

Are you mindful that what you think you're capable of doing can serve to limit you on how you view yourself (your self-concept)? "So, if you have a poor self-concept, then you are likely to be the kind of person to attain" normal "goals, your approach to life is all about" getting by, "and your standards of success are just" good enough.

Suppose you have a very high self-concept, though. In that case, you are more likely to be the sort of person that expects more of yourself, has high aspirations and ambitions, is flexible, and is constantly looking for opportunities to develop and challenge yourself.

How do you ask that?
Your self-concept includes your self-esteem, and your self-esteem depends on whether you think you are willing to deal with problems and whether you think you are capable and capable. So, the kind of person who will still do better because they feel that they are up to the challenge and deserve better incentives and results is a person with a strong self-concept and self-esteem.

So the dilemma is you're NEVER going to go past your self-concept, but the alternative is ... To increase your self-concept, you can Boost your self-esteem so that you can do more in life.

To get started, here are seven simple and useful tips:

1. Accept for yourself
It's not the past that needs to equal the future. Know that your actions were the product of the experience, convictions, and principles you were told to believe. So if you swap those that are unsupportive for those that are helpful, you will naturally start making choices that produce positive and advantageous outcomes. Then you can let go of the past and take constructive steps and move on if you embrace yourself where you are right now. You should not feel guilty, upset, or frustrated anymore because you realize the future is bright as you have matured from your mistakes.

2. Earn self-esteem for yourself
You can't buy or steal self-esteem, just win it, and the good news is, you have the experience and expertise to win your

high self-esteem. It comes from taking on new challenges and exploring development prospects. Do something that you usually wouldn't do, such as charitable or voluntary service, dive into a new sport, or give your support to help accomplish someone else's goals. You're going to be shocked by how simple this move is, and when you offer ... The world will make sure you get there (and I will surely vouch for that).

3. Healthy mind-healthy body
It's been said repeatedly, but the foundation of healthy physical and mental well-being is exercise. Feed right, prevent the environment from toxins, and make sure you sweat! The more it is, the stronger! And ideally, for a sport you like, including swimming, biking, walking, climbing, the list goes on! The more you exert energy, the more you get in return.

This one is difficult to describe ... But trust me that it works. Imagine how exhausted you are after sitting all day on the sofa watching TV compared to a day when you were healthy, like playing with kids in the local park ... How are we made to feel alive by the latter?

4. Be the person you want to be
Most people are waiting to Get, and then they're going to do what they need to do to BE the guy they want to be... But the bad thing is that hoping for the future to roll along, people still live in expectation, and they never get there. There's a feeling here... let's turn it around, instead of...

Why don't we be the person we want to be, and do the stuff we need to do, because we're going to get the stuff we want eventually. If we live the way we want to live now, rather than looking for the right time, could you imagine how amazing we sound and how perfect we are? Can you think what our self-esteem would do to do this? Then what are you going to wait for?

5. Manage the divisive persons in your life

I say handle because we can't stop them often, since they can be people from our families, jobs, or friends' circle. Misery involves enterprise, and pessimistic persons will not want you to have a new lease on life when they sometimes feel left behind. Negativity is like weeds-it takes no effort to cultivate it, and that's why you have to ensure that you carefully manage them in your garden (your environment).

6. Forgive some ... Forgive some

Do not mistake this with being frail, please. Forgiving doesn't mean you condone it, but it means letting go of it. Release the bad thoughts, not someone else, when they hold YOU down.

It's like drinking poison to hang onto bad thoughts and hope that the other party dies. It festers in your body and, instead, harms you. Emotions that do not serve you are vengeance, rage, and envy. Be involved with excitement, intent, compassion, and affection to replace them.

7. Treat it as if it were YOUR life

And your life is yours. Not by your parents. Not from your kids. Not by your girlfriend. And not societies. There is no one-size-fits-all life, except YOURS. Not everyone will agree on how you are living your life, so don't think about their acceptance. You will be like a puppy chasing its tail forever if you live your life to please others.

Assessing the Self-Esteem of a Youngster: Five questions

There are five questions regarding the self-esteem appraisal of an infant or teenager. In all of these, a kid with poor self-esteem would have problems. In evaluating management and care, responses to these questions and findings may be useful.

Question 1 of 5: Measuring the Self-Esteem of a Youngster
How do you think that she (or he) sees her appearance and skills?

Having difficulties with their body appearance is not unusual; our bodies stick with us for life. The body is the direct relation of a human with the outside world and the only aspect of a person that can be seen, heard, and touched by others.

As for her physical presence, is she confident? If she's not happy, is the concern a real one, maybe even one that could be resolved (like crooked teeth)? Or is her struggle with her beauty mainly just in her view, such as a pretty girl thinking she's hideous somehow?

When it comes to appearance and physical features, should she set herself down? What is the essence of her fears and complaints?

Does she feel up to the challenge of comparing herself and her skills to peers of age and grade?

Football is another field that shows the talents or absence of a youngster. In this place, how is she? Competitive activities such as soccer and Little League join a child's life early on and carry on for years through school and non-school programs and events. The need to win is anything but fun for some youngsters.

Question 2 of 5: Measuring the Self-Esteem of a Youngster
How good is manual frustration doing?

Before he loses it, will he take it quite a bit? Can he use defeats strategically as a challenge to work even harder, or is he excessively prone to aggravation and defeats?

It's easy to understand how a frustrated youngster's actions will have repercussions that only cause more anger as the repercussions are introduced. The disappointed child finds himself in a pit that just goes deeper, then deeper still, in one direction.

If self-esteem is a jar by which our tension is handled, some people bear containers, and others have thimbles. During periods of frustration, you can size them up quickly. Put another way, and low anger tolerance is almost certainly a tip-off of low self-esteem.

Question 3 of 5: Measuring the Self-Esteem of a Youngster
How is dissent, even critical, well-intended criticism, handled?

"Does she graciously embrace criticism and use it for change as a springboard, or does just about ANY criticism bring on an answer like," How come you still pick on ME?

For the remainder of their life, some youths believe they have fulfilled their limit of errors for a long time! So, if one more human is kept up in front of them, they're not satisfied with it. The contrary effect also happens. This is the boy who had trouble receiving compliments—a part of the same problem in this case.

We all have a view of ourselves as a full person. If the picture is a bad one, it will clash with congratulations. In other words, the compliment may not find a place to "suit." Accordingly, to preserve continuity with a poor self-image and low self-esteem, the youth might refuse a compliment. This is self-defeating, one might say, and it doesn't make any sense at all, but it's consistent.

Question 4 of 5: Measuring the Self-Esteem of a Youngster
Is it important to take reasonable risks?

The danger is involved in life. The very prospect of change, just about any sort of development, requires that we take risks, not fool-hearted risks, of course, but risks that are suitable for age and circumstance.

Sports and other competitive fields, the type of courses a high school student signs up for or tries for the first after-school job, are examples of threats. Then there is the big one for a man asking for a date for a girl out. Life all the time needs risk. The risk-taking bottom line is still the same: fear of loss. If the fear is sufficiently high, there will be no chance. But it does have a paradoxical consistency. Since success will not be accomplished Until paralyzing terror inevitably produces further disappointment.

A pattern of opposite results could be considered here: the apprehension of achievement. A bad self-image or low self-esteem doesn't mesh in with the entire notion of achievement. Instead of a good life-style, more young people would aspire for the consistency of a bad self-image. That appears to run counter to personality rules, but I've seen it repeatedly happen in more than three decades of interacting with young people.

Question 5 of 5: Assessing the Self-Esteem of a Youngster
How does she cope with interactions, both with friends and with adults?

Does she appear to have many significant friendships, friendships in which she is involved, and lasted? Does she talk with adults quickly and comfortably?

We see young people at the other end, who feel socially alienated and withdrawn. They could say something like, "No one loves me!" They could easily even make friends, but they have trouble holding them.

This youngster could either be awkward with adults or waste their time, like a favorite tutor, with only one friend or one parent. This may seem to be a very good friend, but avoidance of other relationships might be the deeper message. Particularly if that one strong relationship falls apart, this can become a huge issue. And usually, if the relationship in its intensity is one-sided, it will inevitably fall apart eventually.

In such an unfortunate situation, there are underlying concerns, such as two kinds of anxiety: the anxiety of closeness and fear of being socially "exposed" For a teenager, a period of growth where friends are such an integral part of psychosocial progress, it is very upsetting to think of being "exposed simply." This youngster might be afraid that they may not like what they see if people come too close. One way to deal with this topic is never to let anyone come too personal, but never. But, just as the risk problem, it is also self-defeating to not let anyone get near.

CONCLUSION

I believe body image is a major issue, especially with teenagers. The media is a huge influence on how teenagers look at themselves. "Marilyn Monroe once said," To all the girls who think you're ugly because your size isn't 0, you are the pretty one. It's the society that is ugly. This quote is really important because it says that society tells you that you are not perfect and that what society feels is beauty is not actually beautiful. Whether they like their looks or not, teens still want something to change in their bodies.

Body image is how you perceive your physical self, including whether you feel desirable and whether others like your appearance. For several people, especially those in their early teens, body image can be related to self-esteem. Throughout history, humans have said that the beauty of a human body is vital. These days, magazines and TV reflect the norms that they believe your body should be. But our body is not always the same as we want it to be. Teens are when they become more aware of media images and celebrities and how other kids look. They can begin to equate themselves to other individuals or the media. This can all affect how we feel about ourselves and our bodies.

Did you ever mention or think about any of this? I'm too tall." "I'm too short." "I'm too thin." "If only I were thinner, taller, had curly hair, straight hair, longer legs, nose smaller, I'd be happier. "Has anyone or yourself put you down due to the way you look?" If so, you are not alone. Teens are going through lots of changes in their bodies. And, when their body changes, so does their self-image. It's not always easy to like every aspect of your body, but it can really drag down your self-esteem when you always concentrate on the negatives. This is why you should always focus on the positives of your body, not the negatives.

Every individual has their own different definition of body image that defines as beautiful or, in some cases, what the media defines as beautiful, meaning to be skinny. Even with the media making advertisements that catch our attention doesn't mean we have to follow what they represent. Body image is not about being skinny, having a healthy skin tone, beautiful smooth hair, etc., but being comfortable in our skin just the way we please. My point is - no matter the definition the media or anybody gives to beautiful body image, simply show them your body.

In our life stage, teenagers are the one who comes across these low self-esteem and insecurities towards their body and to themselves. It is a perfectly natural stage of life that every single one of them must face. It is also a development stage to know our body and discover who we are and what we hope to gain.

Made in the USA
Coppell, TX
25 February 2021

50860567R00066